Last Call
of the Gods

A Novel

DAVID SAHADI

• Canada • UK • Ireland • USA •

Note for Librarians: A cataloguing record for this book is available from Library and Archives Canada at www.collectionscanada.ca/amicus/index-e.html
ISBN 1-4120-8010-X

Printed in Victoria, BC, Canada. Printed on paper with minimum 30% recycled fibre. Trafford's print shop runs on "green energy" from solar, wind and other environmentally-friendly power sources.

Offices in Canada, USA, Ireland and UK

This book was published *on-demand* in cooperation with Trafford Publishing. On-demand publishing is a unique process and service of making a book available for retail sale to the public taking advantage of on-demand manufacturing and Internet marketing. On-demand publishing includes promotions, retail sales, manufacturing, order fulfilment, accounting and collecting royalties on behalf of the author.

Book sales for North America and international:
Trafford Publishing, 6E–2333 Government St.,
Victoria, BC V8T 4P4 CANADA
phone 250 383 6864 (toll-free 1 888 232 4444)
fax 250 383 6804; email to orders@trafford.com
Book sales in Europe:
Trafford Publishing (UK) Limited, 9 Park End Street, 2nd Floor
Oxford, UK OX1 1HH UNITED KINGDOM
phone 44 (0)1865 722 113 (local rate 0845 230 9601)
facsimile 44 (0)1865 722 868; info.uk@trafford.com
Order online at:
trafford.com/05-3008

10 9 8 7 6 5 4 3 2

Last Call of the Gods

Introduction

Summer 2004

ONE YEAR AGO, life was good. Very good. Or so I thought.

An award-winning Creative Director for a renowned global entertainment company, I was esteemed by my peers in the film and television industry. My job paid handsomely. I drove nice cars, lived in a beautiful house in the Connecticut countryside and dined wherever I wished. And I was fortunate to be blessed with a small circle of true friends.

Then I quit my job and walked away from it all. Just like that. Without warning, and with very serious doubts, I turned my back on the world I had created and knew so well. Was I scared? Absolutely. Did I have a clue as to what I wanted to do? Absolutely not! What I knew for certain was that, like many of you, I was suffering from the soul sickness of modern society.

We live in an age where there is a premium placed on the material. Our culture emphasizes youth, appearances and possessions. Our house is never big enough; we can always use more money and a new car. Each morning we awake, leap out of bed, and frantically jump right back into the never-ending rat race. Our minds still spin like mice in a wheel when we sleep. If, that is, we can truly sleep. What we lack today is a profound belief system of enduring value like generations past.

I had reached a point in my life where this world of pretense and superficiality lost its appeal. I felt empty. My life was lacking purpose. I no longer saw the world through the eyes of a child, awed and inspired by the simple wonders of life itself. My soul needed to embark on a journey of discovery. My spirit longed for adventure. I was determined to find the true joy of life.

When I walked out of my office for the last time, it seemed the weight of the world lifted from my shoulders. Immediately I felt lighter, energized, liberated. I sold my house and most of my belongings, packed what few mementoes I decided to keep in my Jeep, and headed west. I didn't have an agenda. There were no grand plans or roadmaps for this next phase of my life. Eschewing logic and reason, ignoring the advice of friends and the compassion of family who thought I was merely "burnt out", I began a spiritual journey using trust as my guide and intuition my navigational system.

Journeying through old western towns and exploring the majestic wilderness of this great country, I was in search of depth and meaning. I knew there was more to life, some profound purpose as to our existence. I spent a week in solitude in The Badlands of South Dakota, hiking by day, sleeping out under a canopy of brilliant white stars by night, completely removed from the world of cars, cell phones and satellite TV. Alone with earth, sleeping amidst the coyotes and the bison and the prairie dogs, I sought to come to grips with my fears of imaginary demons lurking in the bushes and the shadows of the night. Far removed from the cacophony of modern technology, I hoped to experience an epiphany, or at least make a deep spiritual connection with all that is real.

With a mind still calcified from years of societal conditioning, deep insight at first eluded me. It wasn't until I stopped searching, stopped trying so hard to find, that the divine force of Life, the Universal Source itself, found me.

The eternal wisdom I discovered – or perhaps more appropriately "rediscovered" – from a timeless place long ago, but not so far away, is set forth in this fictional tale. It all unfolds one magical night in a small-town bar in the middle of nowhere. It's a rather modest place. Or so it seems...

Until the gods show up.

Why do we look with ignorance
upon the deaf, dumb and blind?

Do the blind not dream visions
of grandeur in the night?

Do the dumb not understand
the healing hands of love?

Do the deaf not hear
the whispers of angels on the wind,
and the voice of God in their hearts?

Chapter 1

THE ROAD FROM Buffalo, Wyoming to Yellowstone National Park is one of the most spectacular drives in the country. Winding through the Big Horn Mountains and into the Powder River Basin, Route 16 meanders through black forests of poplar and pine. Far in the distance snow-capped mountain peaks, dramatically backlit by vaulted blue skies, embrace traces of mist that caress their slopes. The road ambles leisurely through these valleys, amidst blue sage and a carpet of yellow wildflowers that rise from the ashen rock and stretch for the heavens above. Driving this majestic road, one is reminded of God's brilliance, and sees a divine presence everywhere.

If, that is, one believes in God.

In silence, save for the sounds of tires racing on asphalt and the wind strafing the Jeep, I pondered on the questions that have weighed heavily on human hearts for eons: Is there a God? What is He/She? Was Jesus really the Son of God, or only the mortal son of man? And what is life's ultimate mystery, the one that eludes human comprehension, yet informs our entire existence? Like our ancestors who for ages asked these questions atop mountains and besides rivers, I heard no answers.

Perhaps I would find spiritual insight at my next destination, Yellowstone National Park. Or have it find me. That's what I hoped.

The minutes passed and the sun dramatically enlarged and reddened as it continued its inexorable journey to the distant horizon, relinquishing Wyoming to the darkness of night to awaken fields in faraway lands. I looked at the clock. It was 7:30. Jackson Hole, my eventual destination, was many hours away. It would be impossible to arrive there until long after dark. I was disappointed. This drive was far too spectacular to relinquish to the black sheath of night.

Easing out of a gently sloping turn with a rolling field of bison, I pulled the Jeep to the side of the road and retrieved an atlas. I truly was in the middle of nowhere. Not a single car had passed for at least twenty minutes. I studied the map, looking at the few small towns that were ahead. Less than an hour's drive was a town called Lander. I had never heard of it, but I liked the town's name. It seemed like a good place to stop.

A bison grunted and a crow squawked in the distance. My stomach growled, too, as if in communication with the creatures of the wilderness. I was suddenly ravenous! Hopefully, there would be a bar in town where I could get a burger, a beer, and watch the playoff game between the New York Yankees and the Boston Red Sox. It was the deciding Game Seven of the American League Championship Series and the drama promised to be intense. Especially since the Yankees had gotten off to a stunning three-games-to-none lead and appeared on their way to the World Series, only to see the Red Sox win three in a row in dramatic fashion. So much for camping and eating trail mix and searching for God in the hot mountains and scorched plains of the desert: tonight, I was going to fully indulge a few of the decadent amenities of modern living, however superficial they may be. I pulled back onto the open highway and continued the journey.

By the time I came to a sign that said *Welcome to Lander, Population 6,686,* the sun had disappeared beneath the distant mountains. The once white clouds lashed out from the horizon like red rivers of flames, consuming the blue sky and leaving purple, then blackness, further east in their wake. I laughed at the irony. Just an hour ago, I looked to the sky and saw heavenly colors. Now, I beheld the fires of hell. Both were equally spectacular.

As I drove down Main Street the quaint shops, restaurants and small businesses that catered to outdoor enthusiasts were bathed in a beautiful crimson hue. Lander seemed more like the innocent TV town of Mayberry than an old Wild West settlement. To the right was a small tavern nestled in an old historic red brick building. I was grateful. A few blocks down was the Lander Motel. A green neon sign flashed "vacancy". From outside appearances the motel seemed modest, but welcoming. I parked, rented a room for just $30, dropped off my duffle bag, and, without even stopping to unpack, walked four blocks to the Lander Tavern and sat right down at the bar.

The bartender was an attractive woman in her late twenties with a lean, shapely body, long brown hair and emerald cat-like eyes. She was the prettiest female I had seen in weeks. I took that as a good omen.

"What brings you to Lander?" she politely asked, placing a coaster in front of me. "Or did it just get in the way?"

"It just got in the way," I smiled, amused at her witty greeting. Really, it was not all that far from the truth.

"That's what they all say," she teased.

I ordered a local micro beer named Red Canyon Ale and scanned the scene. The atmosphere was an eclectic blend of modern times and the nostalgia of wild days long since gone. The huge seasoned oak bar dominated the room, separating a small section with wooden tables and chairs behind me from a more lively area with two pool tables, a dart board, and a jukebox near the rear. Mounted on red brick walls were two televisions, along with several trophy heads of moose, elk, bison and mountain deer. Mixed among the mounted game were old pictures of the Wild West, as well as photos of sports heroes past and present. I was extremely heartened to see a black-and-white photo of a professional wrestler named Classy Freddie Blassie, a colorful character who wrestled for five decades from the forties through the eighties. I doubted he had ever been here, in this humble, remote town. The bar's owner was probably a fan.

In the religion known as professional wrestling, fans came to the arenas, their holy temples, for two reasons: to cheer passionately for their favorite heroes – who they revered as gods – and to hope and pray that the evil ones, known as "heels", suffer defeat. Freddie

Blassie was a great heel, probably the most hated wrestler who ever lived. And he won most of his matches, too, which only further enraged the congregation who cursed him. Twenty one times he was stabbed by crazed fans. Once, he even had acid thrown on his face. All the while, Freddie Blassie taunted the fans with a colorful barrage of insults. He loved every moment he played the role of bad guy.

I smiled broadly as I stared at his photo. Not only was he a great showman and entertainer, but in real life he truly was a classy gentleman and benevolent soul. And more importantly, he was a dear, personal friend. Sadly, just three months ago, I witnessed his passing, watching as this once fearless man reluctantly surrendered to death in a hospital room at the age of eighty-six. His wife, Miyako, was present, as well as a neighbor named Jerome. That was all. None of his children were there, nor his grandchildren, nor anyone from the wrestling federation where he had given so much of his heart and soul and spent much of his career. It was just the three of us, hoping, crying and praying in vain.

Posing with his championship belt in the photo, Freddie Blassie was once again a youthful picture of strength and indestructibility. It was an image I'd prefer to remember him by, rather then the withered old body and scared soul that lay helplessly on his death bed.

"Good to see you again, you Old Bastard!" I said quietly, raising my glass in toast. I called him an 'Old Bastard' as a term of endearment; he called me a 'No-Good Piece of Shit.' That meant he really liked me. One would have to know Freddie to understand that.

On a TV set mounted high above the far side of the bar the baseball game caught my attention. A die-hard Yankees' fan, I was thrilled. It was a tradition passed on by my dad, who often extolled the virtues of the great Joe DiMaggio. And this promised to be a game for the ages. Not only was this the greatest rivalry in sports, but it was also October baseball. Tonight, this epic battle would determine which team would go to the World Series. The drama could not be any more intense. I was hoping the famed "Curse of the Bambino" would break the hearts of the Boston faithful at least one more time. The Curse had lived since 1918, and lived well.

I took a satisfying swig of ale and turned to my right. Two seats down in the very corner sat a rather unusual man of fifty, or perhaps sixty. It was hard to tell since his hair was cut extremely short, barely longer than stubble. His expression seemed one of calm, his demeanor gentle and introspective. I couldn't tell if he was a regular local or a fellow journeyman like me just passing through town. One thing certain was that looked quite content in his current situation, whatever that may be. An aura of peacefulness enveloped him, like a gentle mist that surrounds a mountaintop on a cool, spring morning. On the bar in front of him was a half bottle of Heineken, which he poured carefully into a short, clear glass. He looked admiringly at the gold brew that bubbled before him and sipped it slowly, ever so diligently, savoring every moment as if it was the last beer he might ever enjoy.

"Does anything interesting ever happen around here?" I asked the quiet stranger.

He turned away from his beer and looked at me with a kind, gentle smile.

"Nothing at all," he replied benignly. "And everything, too," he added.

"Sounds like a contradiction."

"You'd be surprised."

"My name is David," I said, offering my hand. He took it in his and smiled.

"I am Budd." Then he released his hand and quietly turned his attention back to his bubbling glass of beer.

Leaving Budd in the comfort of his solitude, I scanned the faces of the other strangers in this unfamiliar bar. On the farthest end from where I sat, stoic and quite even amongst themselves, sat three Native Americans, their long black hair pulled back in ponytails, their faces adorned with apparent disenchantment and despair. I remembered driving through the Wind River Indian Reservation on my ride into town and knew Lander was close to sacred land.

Sacred land. What was so scared about this land? What hallowed secrets did she reveal to the Native Americans, but not to me? I momentarily withdrew from the game and the ambience of this strange yet comforting bar and once again ruminated on life's great mysteries. And I was frustrated with my lack of knowing.

I was raised a Catholic and studied many of the world's great religions in college. The lessons brought ideological knowledge but no clear insight. Nor did the countless New Age books I read that attempted to explain the unexplainable.

I also remembered a traditional Buddhist axiom that said, "When the student is ready, the teacher will appear." Well, I quit my job, sold everything I owned, and braved the barren wilderness in an unknown land. Damn it, if I wasn't ready, who was?

Suddenly, the music brought me right back to the present moment, as if someone in the bar had screamed my name, snapping me out of a trance. I looked around.

The jukebox bellowed the melodic song, *"Personal Jesus."* And then amidst the crowd I beheld an impossible sight!

I coughed up beer in shock and disbelief. My eyes widened and my heart nearly stopped! Wiping my mouth with eyes wide open, I stared with amazement at the odd fellow sitting halfway down the bar dressed in a beige cloak with blue tassels and a white linen tunic underneath. He looked like the very embodiment Jesus Christ! And no one else seemed to notice.

"Your own, personal Jesus," crooned the voice from the jukebox. *"Someone to hear your prayers, someone who's there."*

He sat amidst a glow of a bright white light, as if he was an actor starring on a Broadway stage. I had the strange sensation that the light emanated from within.

"Feeling unknown and you're all alone, flesh and bone, by the telephone," the song decreed. I couldn't believe what I was seeing.

"Pick up the receiver; I'll make you a believer."

There was no denying the fact that he had an immutable presence. I continued to stare, trying to ascertain who or what I was really seeing. Was it an apparition? A strange trick of the light? Some mislaid soul performing a magician's tricks of illusions? If you are indeed Jesus Christ, acknowledge me right now! At that precise moment, he turned toward me, made deep, purposeful contact with penetrating eyes, and winked.

I left my seat and walked quickly to the men's room. This can't be happening! But, hard as I tried to rationalize the seeming apparition I just beheld, something deep inside told me an extraordinary event was going on here. I just knew it.

I splashed cold water on my face, wiped it dry, and looked directly in the mirror. Everything seemed OK with my appearance. There was color in my skin, too much perhaps. My eyes weren't dilated. My tongue wasn't swollen. There were no visible signs of heat exhaustion or dehydration, and I knew I wasn't drunk. Pinching myself for good measure, pretending to make sure I wasn't having a dream, I anxiously decided to return to my seat at the bar. As I regained the courage to leave the bathroom, the hair was raised on the back of my neck and goose bumps were spawning on my arms.

When I returned he was gone. So was the bright light under which he sat. The song was still playing on the jukebox. It must be an extended play. I breathed a large sigh of relief. Perhaps it really was just an illusion, a trick of the eye. I sat down and resumed my place near the corner of the bar next to Budd. He gave an innocent nod of his head and smiled. Feeling calm once again, I took a healthy swig of ale.

"Is this seat taken?" asked a voice to my immediate left.

I turned and instantly my eyes widened and my breathing stopped and my heart tried to leap out of my throat.

It was He!

Really He!

And now He was sitting directly beside me!

I dropped my glass. The beer spilled all over his garment. He didn't flinch, nor get the least bit annoyed. Surprisingly, the glass did not break. Instead, it bounced off the floor, and, like a rubber ball, bounced back high into His waiting clutch. Gently, He handed it to me. I looked at the stain on His clothes. As I watched in awe, the beer on His garment dried within seconds and the stain completely disappeared.

For what seemed like an eternity I couldn't articulate a single word, much less a thought. All the while He just looked at me with calm countenance and smiled. Oddly, I was no longer frightened. Now, I was bewildered, deeply in awe, trying to grasp the truth before me, trying to make sense of what was happening. Finally, my voice found its courage and I was able to speak.

"Are you...?"

"I am," He quickly answered.

"You are who?" I asked with a voice still trembling. I didn't want to appear foolish and invoke the name Jesus, lest He was a mere mortal and thought I was crazy.

"I am that I am."

"The actual Son of..."

"We are all sons and daughters of God," He kindly interjected.

In the very marrow of my being I knew it was indeed He, Jesus of Galilee, the Holy Messiah, the one who died on the cross for the sins of mankind. He was tall and lean with long brown hair and eyes of yellow-green. His skin was weathered and bronzed. His nose was bigger and His lips fuller than most modern depictions of Christ. I smiled faintly at the random notion that He bore no resemblance to Jim Caveziel, the actor who played Jesus in Mel Gibson's film, *The Passion of The Christ.*

"That was a lousy job of casting," He quipped, obviously reading my thoughts.

Around His being was a discernible blue-white glow, as if, like a human firefly, He radiated light. His bright aura seemed to stretch and envelop me as well, bathing my spirit with deep, soothing feelings of calm and warmth, filling me with a great sense of peace.

I looked at His hands. The center of His palms bore the scars where metal spikes had once bound him to the wooden cross.

"Kind of ironic, isn't it?" He said.

"What's that?" I asked not knowing, my mind still mesmerized and awed by His presence.

"Do you know what I did for a living?"

"You were a preacher," I answered.

"Before that. I didn't start my ministry until I was thirty."

"Were you a shepherd?"

"Good guess. Most prophets were. But not me."

"What did you do?"

"I was a carpenter. And I died nailed to a wooden cross. Do you see the irony?"

"Now I do."

"Now you'll never forget it."

I resumed my examination of His physical appearance. Atop His head was the proverbial crown of thorns. Scabs of dried blood were present at the points of impact where the thorns penetrated His scalp. Why was He wearing it now? Perhaps it was just for effect.

"It is for effect," He replied, again reading my

thoughts. "I tend to be a little dramatic from time to time. It always gets one's attention."

He removed the crown from His head and flipped it like a Frisbee toward the front door. It whistled as it flew through the air, gently landing on the hat rack. No one in the bar seemed to notice what He just did. Not even the stranger beside me, who continued to stare admiringly at his beer. It seemed I was the only one who was aware of this divine presence.

"How can this be possible?" I asked.

"Anything is possible."

"In Wyoming?"

"As I've preached many times, with the power of God nothing's impossible. Or to use a twenty-first century colloquialism, 'Impossible Is Nothing!' That is the new addidas slogan, is it not? Quite a clever twist on the old adage."

"Why are you here?" I asked.

The smile vanished from His face. He looked down, then away. His shoulders dropped and His head hung low. The whitish glow that emanated from His being momentarily diminished, as if someone had lowered the fader switch on a lamp. He appeared distraught. Then He let out a deep sigh and raised His head to speak.

"I am saddened."

"Saddened?"

"You might say depressed."

"What is depressing you?"

"All that is going on in the world."

"What in particular?"

"Misunderstanding."

"I'm not sure I fully understand."

"That's my point. No one does. I am misunderstood, as are my teachings."

I was dumbfounded. The message of Jesus Christ misunderstood? Christianity was the world's biggest monotheistic religion. Millions of faithful followers lived by His word, some with great fervor. Some even sacrificed their lives in belief of His word.

"And the lives of others," He added, the sound of regret in His voice.

"How so?"

"My teachings are of Love, tolerance, and selflessness. I preached the virtues of mercy and forgiveness. I spoke of eternity, of life everlasting. But over the centuries my teachings have been twisted, contaminated and corrupted by humanity. They have been stained by powerful, money-seeking bureaucrats, tainted by misguided clergymen who lost the way, entangled in a sickening web of religious and military alliances. Over the millennia, Man has used my teachings to murder and maim, to wage horrific wars and wipe out entire civilizations. Look at the Holy Wars, The Crusades, the Spanish Inquisition, and the Protestant Reformation that nearly tore Europe apart. And it still continues today in Northern Ireland and the Middle East. Throughout history more people have been murdered in the name of Christianity than all of the conventional World Wars combined."

He paused for a moment to let the anger that seemed to grow in him subside. Then He spoke in a tone of sorrow.

"I spoke of Love and man has since used my words to incite hate. I spoke of Giving and man has since used my teachings to validate taking. I spoke of Unity and man has used my message to divide. I spoke of Life and man has since used my name to justify killing and death. Indeed, I am misunderstood."

He became silent. Still bewildered by His presence, and feeling incapable of consoling Him, I sat in silence, too. Glancing around the bar, I noticed that every one carried on as if it was business as usual, lost in what now seemed to be trifling worlds of gossip, pool-playing and drinking. They were completely unaware of the presence of the Holy One lamenting His sorrows in their bar. I wished I could think of something to do to help ease His burdens.

The bartender stopped by and I asked Jesus if He wanted a drink. His aura brightened, and He nodded affirmatively. I ordered myself another ale. Jesus addressed the bartender directly.

"Hello Jennifer," He said.

"Hi Jay. Haven't seen you in a while."

"I've been busy."

"Doing what?"

"Trying to save the world."

She laughed. I had the feeling that He was completely serious while she had no idea of the depths of His statement.

"What are you drinking tonight?" she asked.

"Wine, please. What kind of red do you have?"

"Cabernet and merlot."

"From where?"

"California."

"Hmmm."

Again He appeared solemn. "I'll just have a Perrier," He replied with resignation. "And a clean wine glass, please."

I turned to Jesus as she walked away. "Why does she call you Jay?" I asked.

"She got that from Mo."

"Who's Mo?"

"You'll meet him. He'll be here soon."

The bartender returned. Immediately, I took a sip of the cold brew to wash away the dryness in my throat. Jesus mumbled something about forgetting to say that He didn't want ice. He asked me to hand him an empty pint glass that was atop the bar. Then He emptied the ice from His glass into the pint and poured the Perrier into His glass. He took a slight sniff of the bubbling water. He looked left, then right. When He was sure no one was watching, He wiped His right hand over His glass of water. Instantly it became red. He cracked a slight smile. Sure enough He had turned His glass of water into wine!

"So, you really can do that?" I asked, astonished.

"But of course," He proudly replied.

"Why Perrier?"

"Why not?"

"You could just order tap water and save some cash, couldn't you?"

He leaned into me, cautiously, as if ready to divulge some divine secret. "The French always made the best wines," He said in a low voice, and smiled.

With a graceful movement He brought the glass to His nose. The aroma brought an even bigger smile to His face. Then He took a slow, gentle sip, and let the wine roll on His tongue a few seconds before swallowing. He let out a soft, satisfying sigh.

"There's a lot of wisdom in a glass of red wine," He remarked. "Not so much in a bottle, though."

"How often do you drink red wine?" I wondered.

"Every night with supper."

"Every night?"

Once again He leaned His head into mine so that no one else in the bar could hear what He was saying. "Sometimes during the afternoon, too," he confessed with a devilish grin.

"I thought drinking every day was bad for you?"

"Excess is bad for you. It kills. So does moderation. It doesn't kill as fast, but perhaps it does so more painfully. Moderation is a prolonged death that slowly eats away at the soul. Responsibility, that's the key. Be responsible for all you do in the world; all your words, all your actions, all your deeds. And know your limits."

Jesus took another sip of wine.

"Plus, I didn't have to worry about drinking when I was preaching," He added.

"Why not?"

"They didn't have DWIs in my day."

His look was one of absolute seriousness. I stared with deep incredulity. Jesus a reckless partyier? It definitely did not fit my perception of one so Holy.

"Just joking!" He laughed, and poked my side with His index finger. "Gotcha! Gotcha good, didn't I?"

I chuckled along with Him, even though I thought He sounded a bit geeky when He said 'Gotcha! Gotcha good!' I was happy, confused, mesmerized, bewildered, anxious, calm, and excited--all at the same time.

"He that is merry of heart hath a continual feast. I was quite the humorist in my day. Split the apostles' sides every night at supper," He informed.

"Really? I never knew you had a comedic side."

"No one does. History is written by the manipulative, the powerful and the conquerors. Those who wrote the Bible three hundred years after my mortal passing thought it would be in their best interests to omit my comedic nature. No wonder it is such a laborious read."

He became solemn again. It appeared His mind returned to some distant pool of sadness. After a quiet moment of introspection, He sighed and nodded His head. Then He spoke again in a serious tone.

"Do you know what else saddens me?" He asked.

"Tell me."

"The way most pastors and priests portray God. It is written in the Bible that, 'God made Man in God's own image.' Nothing can be further from the truth. It is Man who made God in Man's image. They have made Him angry and vengeful. They have attached human emotions to Him when God is above human emotions.

31

They conjure up images of an angry white-haired man sitting in the clouds tossing lightning bolts down at the sinful. How sad. God is All-Loving and All-Merciful, never judgmental. He is not bound by physical or temporal limitations. We dishonor God and compromise His infinite power and efficacy for our own good when we reduce Him to such grossly mistaken portrayals. God is Spirit, and we must worship Him in spirit, love and truth.

"I am also saddened by all those who warn of the Second Coming and speak of the Final Resurrection as a future event. They should realize that my spirit never left and that I am already here in the now, if only they will open their hearts.

"And lastly, I never intended a ministry to be founded that idolized and worshipped me. After all, it is not my word I spoke but the Word of God. I delivered a beautiful and blessed message, but one should not forget that I was merely the messenger, not the creator of the message. There is one true Creator in the universe. The divine spark of God exists within every living creature on earth. And the gates of Heaven are open to all."

He looked upward. "I delight to do thy will, my God; thy law is within my heart."

From the jukebox the Dylan classic, "*Knocking on*

Heaven's Door" began playing. I chuckled at the irony. And I noticed that the precise moment the song began His eyes brightened and His aura grew.

"He's here," He proclaimed with seeming joy.

"Who?" I asked.

"One of The Others. It's about time. He's late."

I turned toward the door and was aghast. Sure enough, I recognized the Holy Man walking straight toward us.

It seemed this unassuming town named Lander was a place where Mayberry meets the Twilight Zone.

Chapter 2

"SAY HEY, JAY," said The Other.

"What's up Mo?" replied Jesus.

The Other gave Jesus a long, heartfelt embrace. When they separated, they patted their right fists on their chests twice before bringing two fingers to their lips and making a peace sign toward the heavens. It looked like a combination Snoop Dog meets Sammy Sosa greeting. Obviously, they were caught up with the cultural trends of the day.

"Assalam o-Aleikum" said The Other.

"Peace be unto you as well, my brother."

I intuitively recognized The Other as the great prophet Muhammad. Like Jesus, a white-blue aura also enveloped his being, and his body had the same ethereal quality. He was wearing a flowing red robe that covered a white tunic underneath. Atop his head was a traditional black turban. He had a long full beard of black that seemed as though it hadn't been groomed for weeks. His skin was dark and he had coffee-bean eyes, and in them, I sensed, was a residue of profound sadness.

"This is David," said Jesus, making our introduction.

"I know," said Muhammad, as he gave me the same fist bump, two-fingered greeting.

"Forgive me," said Jesus. "Of course you do. How are you holding up?"

"Not well. The Bombers are at it again." With a look of sadness he raised his head towards the television. To my delight, the Bronx Bombers, a.k.a. the New York Yankees, had taken a 2-0 lead against the Red Sox in the top of the third. The bases were loaded with only one out and they were threatening to score more. The great Pedro Martinez was flirting with trouble and the Red Sox were in a jam.

"Are you a Red Sox fan?" I asked Muhammad.

"What sacrilege!" he snapped, turning his head to confront me. "I am one of the Yankee faithful. What on earth made you think I rooted for the Red Sox?"

"Well, you seemed upset when you said 'the Bombers are at it again'."

"Not those Bombers – the suicide bombers in the Middle East" He appeared annoyed at my misunderstanding, but it quickly passed, replaced by apparent sorrow. "You'll see it on TV in a few minutes," he informed.

With a somber look on his face he turned back to Jesus. "There are going to be coordinated attacks in Baghdad, Riyadh, and Kabul. Three different cities in three different countries and they will all be hit at approximately the same time by suicide truck bombers. That's a first. And they are going to use dirty bombs. That's another first. Nearly two thousand will be killed, thousands more injured, millions filled with fear. The carnage will be gross, and, like you, I am powerless to prevent it."

"It's getting worse," lamented Jesus.

"Yes. The chasm is widening. Humanity may be nearing a point of no return."

Jesus shook His head in disappointment. For a brief moment, His glow dimmed. "They should take up writing, or preaching, instead of dying," said Jesus.

"I always said the ink of the scholar is more holy than the blood of the martyr," responded Muhammad.

"You did, Mo. Your message was quite clear."

"Clear, yes. Heeded? No. The so-called Holy War being waged by the militant extremists today goes against the very essence of Islam. It is an affront to Muslims everywhere."

After the events of September 11th I briefly embarked on a literary exploration of the religion of Islam. I was searching for answers as to why the extremists had declared a Holy War on the United States of America. They also invoked the names of Allah and Muhammad in their crusade. It didn't seem believable to me that their God and great prophet would speak of hate and justify such horrifying acts of aggression.

"Islam is against aggression. All forms of aggression," Muhammad informed me. Apparently he, too, could read my mind. "Sanction is giving for war only in self defense."

Muhammad emphasized that Islam teaches that all men are equal before God. There is no prejudice, either by race or color, and no distinction between Arabs and non-Arabs. Goodness is the only criterion of worth. And charity is a duty unto every Muslim.

"He who hath not the means thereto, let him do a good act or abstain from an evil one. That is his charity," Muhammad said. "But the Islamic terrorists of this world ignore this very tenant of Islamic faith. The extremists are misguided, committing evil acts upon their brothers, killing in the name of Allah, when the Almighty and Merciful would wish for no such thing."

He paused for a moment to quell his apparent growing rage. When his aura brightened, he continued.

"When I revealed the word of God in the Koran, Arabia was in a state of religious chaos. The Arabs were steeped in ignorance and constantly at war with one another. They worshiped idols, stars and stones. They oppressed the poor and the meek. They belittled women. I proclaimed the glory of God, denounced their evil ways, and called them to a better way of life, one of humility, tolerance, compassion and religious enthusiasm. I was the biggest advocate of women's rights, too, bestowing upon them spiritual and material equality with man. Fifteen hundred years later, again there is religious chaos and political dissolution. Fifteen hundred years later, women are once again oppressed in many Muslim societies. Fifteen hundred years later, Muslims are killing Jews, Muslims are killing Christians, Muslims are killing Muslims. The teachings of the Koran have been twisted by these misguided souls to incite and inflame instead of to heal, to kill instead of breathe the sweet air of compassion into life. It fills me with such despair."

Muhammad shook his head and looked away. I thought he might be concealing a tear.

"You look like you can use a drink," noted Jesus.

"As you know, drinking is forbidden in Islam," Muhammad reminded. "But tonight is one of those nights that truly tests one's discipline."

"Allow me to buy," I offered.

"Thank you, brother. That is a kind act of charity." Muhammad then turned to Jesus and looked at his glass. "What do you have going on there, Jay?" he asked.

"Red. From France." He offered his glass to Muhammad. "Try it. It's mighty fine, if I may say so myself."

Muhammad took Jesus' glass in his hand and raised it just underneath his nose. He twirled the wine gently, softly, and slightly inhaled. Then he handed the glass back to Jesus without taking a sip.

"What an amazing nose. That's an excellent vintage."

"Thank you."

"You're at it again, aren't you Jay?"

Jesus humbly nodded.

I retrieved cash from my wallet to pay for a round. The bartender swiftly came by and indulged me in conversation.

"So, I see you've made some friends," she noted.

"I have."

"They are good guys. Never start any trouble. Good tippers, too."

"I would like to buy Muhammad a drink."

"Who?" she asked, puzzled. With my thumb I pointed to the great Muslim prophet behind me.

She turned and addressed Muhammad. "The usual, Mo? Cranberry and Seven Up?" she asked.

"No," replied Muhammad, "I'll have a glass of wine."

"Wine? I'm shocked. You never drink."

"I know. But I'm afraid it's going to be one of those nights."

"White? Red?"

"The same one Jay is drinking."

Her face turned to a scowl. "Jay is drinking Perrier," she said with absolute conviction.

"Perrier? No, it is wine."

Jesus kicked Muhammad in the shin. He grimaced for an instant, than realized his faux pas.

"Oh, yes, I meant a Perrier. Sorry for the confusion, my dear."

"Would you like a glass, too?"

"Please."

Jesus leaned to Muhammad and whispered in his ear.

"Oh, and hold the ice," Muhammad ordered, on Jesus' recommendation.

When she returned with his drink Muhammad poured the Perrier into a glass. Then he brought it close to himself, just below his chest, concealing it from the views of the patrons. Jesus looked left, then right. When He was sure no one was watching He once again wiped His right hand over the glass of bubbling water. Instantly, it was transformed into red wine.

Muhammad started to take a sip, then stopped.

"On second thought Jay, I will not give in to temptation. I want to maintain a good example. It is the duty of a leader, I believe. Can you please change it back to Perrier?"

"But of course." With another quick swipe of his hand the red libation was changed back to clear, bubbling water.

I looked around at the crowd. No one noticed the minor miracles, or even seemed to be paying attention to us. They appeared lost in private worlds, like bugs on a leaf, aware only of the surface upon which they crawled, oblivious to the divine presence that was in the bar. Except, that is, for the quiet man to my right who was nursing his Heineken. For the first time I noticed he seemed to be quietly conscious of all that was happening, even sensitive to my feelings of awe and bewilderment. At that moment he turned and looked at me with a warmth and gentleness in his eyes as if he was trying to elicit a question, hoping, I sensed, to receive an inquiry he might be able to answer.

"Do you know who these guys are?" I asked, pointing to Jesus and Muhammad behind me, now engaged in a serious conversation about the events unfolding in the Middle East.

"Yes," he replied.

"Jesus and Muhammad!" I proclaimed with a sense of startle and glee, not knowing if he truly knew.

"Indeed. They come here often.

"How often?"

"Whenever they are troubled."

"Are they often troubled?"

"Lately, quite often."

I looked around at the crowd. They were still indifferent, carrying on with apparent incomprehension.

"Does anyone else in this place know who they are?"

"No."

"How can that be?"

"People see only what they wish to see. Or what their logical minds allow them to accept."

"Do they not see them at all?"

"They see them, but not the way you and I do."

"What do they see?"

"A man who looks like a hippie, wearing a white shirt, and his friend with a long beard, red sweater and a midnight blue baseball cap atop his head. And if I'm not mistaken, I think it bears the insignia of the New York Yankees."

I smiled at the irony. The great Muhammad emerges in the middle of Wyoming in the twenty-first century and appears as a mere baseball fan to the oblivious few in the bar. I chuckled to myself as I imagined in silence the booming voice of the Yankee Stadium public address announcer, Bob Sheppard. *'Now batting for the New York Yankees, Muhammad!'*

"How do you know this?" I asked.

"I just do," replied Budd. I didn't question the source of his knowledge. Soon, I engaged Budd on the subject of Islam. He told me that Muhammad was born in Mecca in 570. His father died before his birth. He had no formal schooling, and earned his living as a shepherd. Thoughtful by nature, this occupation enabled him to commune with creation and contemplate the great mysteries of life. Whenever the iniquities of his people oppressed him, he would retire to the solitude of a cave to meditate and commune with the Invisible Power that fills the universe. Eventually, he would spend the entire month of Ramadan there.

It was during one of these retreats that Muhammad heard the voice of God calling him to go forth and preach. He felt as if the words spoken to his soul had been written on his heart. At first he preached only to his immediate friends and relatives. When he did go forth to the masses and denounced the idolatry of his people and their evil ways, he was subject to violence and persecution. His enemies claimed he was mad, a man gone insane. His adversaries attempted many times to kill him. He lived in oppression. Eventually, his followers grew strong, and two decades later Islam spread exponentially and the conversion of the Arabs was complete. While on this earth, Muhammad was humble and of devout mind. He lived in great humility, performing the most menial of tasks on a daily basis. He even cobbled his own shoes. His moral teachings sprang from an exalted mind aflame with religious enthusiasm and carrying a purity of spirit.

"Such indeed was the generosity of his good works that he died in debt," Budd stated, ending the brief history lesson on Muhammad.

Suddenly, my attention was drawn to the television. The baseball game was interrupted by a news flash concerning the bombings in Baghdad, Riyadh and Kabul, the ones Muhammad had earlier prophesized. Where moments ago pictures of grown men playing a young boy's game had been showcased, images of bombed buildings, burning cars and injured people now occupied the screen. The sounds of bat hitting ball and leather catching rawhide, of crowds cheering, and the imagined smells of peanuts, hot dogs and Cracker Jack, were now replaced by the sounds of horrified screams and desperate sirens, and the palpable aroma of death.

Jesus and Muhammad turned their attentions to the screen. Then they lowered their heads and sadly looked away, and, I believe, said a silent prayer.

How did Muhammad know what was going to happen? As soon as I thought I quickly found the answer to my own question. Of course he could predict the future: he's a god.

"My friend, I am not God." Muhammad raised his head and stared deliberately into my eyes, a piercing look of seriousness clearly etched on his face. "Nor am I 'a god'. I am merely a messenger of Allah, the One who is Eternal, Indivisible, Almighty, All-Knowing, Just Merciful, Loving and Forgiving. My God is the same God as my brother Jesus, the same God as the Hebrews. The heavenly message that came to Moses also came to me. The same teachings of Jesus I also embrace and preach. But I am not God. The Voice of The Divine merely uses our lips to be heard. The Will of

God merely uses our bodies to spread His word across the land."

"I'm sorry. I didn't know."

"Ignorance is indeed a dangerous weapon," he said. Then he patted me on the shoulder and smiled. "Of course, you are forgiven."

What a strange night. My head was spinning like a hurricane. Two of the world's greatest religious figures, two immortal prophets, were engaging me in discussion. It was impossible to fathom, but indeed it was happening. And I even had a witness sitting beside me to confirm it.

Once again, the music from the jukebox grabbed my attention. This time for a very weird reason. The song now playing was the traditional Jewish wedding song called, *Hava Nigila*. How bizarre. What is such a song even doing on a jukebox? Especially in this bar in the middle of Wyoming? Then again, everything that was happening tonight was bizarre and defied logic. The world, it seemed, was turning upside down and spinning in many directions at once.

I felt a cool rush of air. I turned towards the front door. My jaw dropped once more as I saw him enter the room.

No longer were two Holy Ones in the Lander Tavern. Now, there were three.

Chapter 3

AS HE ENTERED, the multitude of patrons standing in the bar with drinks in hand parted, oblivious to his divine presence, moving away without even thinking as he approached, as if guided by an unseen force, like the cloud pushed by the invisible wind or a stick caught in the outgoing tide.

I turned to Budd, seeking confirmation as to the identity of this divine being. He was already nodding his head in anticipation of my question. It was indeed the man who set the Jewish people free, led them out of Egypt, gave them their laws and founded their religion. Moses was in the house!

His aura appeared dimmer than that of Jesus and Muhammad. I wasn't sure if it was because he was older, weaker, or perhaps just angry. A scowl was clearly etched on his face. I noticed the bright light of the gods dimmed slightly when they displayed sadness or anger. Even the enlightened ones, it seems, were bound to their inescapable humanity by the strong, confining chains of human emotions from time to time.

"How are you, Mose?" posed Jesus.

"Not well. It's awful what's happening in the world."

"I know," said Muhammad. "We all share deep pain. But try to be strong. Stay in the Light. Have faith that eventually they will see the Light, too."

Moses looked at me. There were deep wells of sadness within his old, tired eyes. His hair was brittle and white, his face etched with scars that were testament to a life of struggle, hardship, persecution and despair. I extended my hand in a formal introduction.

"This is David," said Muhammad.

"I know," snapped Moses.

"Forgive me. Of course you do."

"Pleased to make you acquaintance, David," he said, grabbing my forearm with his palm in an old-fashioned Roman handshake. "I just wish it was under better circumstances."

The three prophets greeted each other with sincere hugs and forearm shakes, and, as they embraced

Moses, I could see his aura brighten and expand. The power of compassion and kindness was evident.

"How can this be?" I asked, turning to Budd. "This evening is so surreal."

"Yet, very real too, my friend," replied Budd. "Try not to question." I noticed that his bottle of Heineken still remained half full. Odd, I thought, since I didn't see him order a beer in the hour or so I had been here. Then again, my head was spinning relentlessly since the moment Jesus arrived and I now possessed a very poor sense of time.

"Why is this happening to me?" I asked Budd.

"You may ask, 'why is this happening to you?' It may not be happening to you at all."

"I just want to understand what's going on."

"You may feel you need to understand everything, but you don't need to understand a thing. Just accept and observe. Then soon, my friend, you may learn."

There was something about this odd fellow that I liked. I sensed a connection on the deepest of levels, as if he was a kindred spirit or a long lost relative or friend. Perhaps even a guardian angel of sorts.

"Angels are real," he said, shocking me with the co-incidence of his statement.

"And there are no coincidences, my friend," he added. I realized at that very moment that he, too, could read my thoughts.

"Can everyone here read my mind?" I asked.

"Only the Holy Ones. And the 'Advanced'."

"The Advanced?"

"You'll soon see. It'll be obvious to spot them."

I turned my attention to the three illustrious religious icons gathered just to my side. They were engaged in a serious conversation. Carefully, I studied Moses, his physical features, the long red robe with vertical white and black stripes that draped his body, and was amused when I realized that he looked just like the actor Charlton Heston who portrayed him in the epic movie, *The Ten Commandments.*

"Cecil B. DeMille did a fine job of casting," Moses said, turning his attention to me, "unlike what that Gibson kid did to my brother Jesus in *The Passion.*"

"At least my movie did better than yours at the box office!" quipped Jesus. Both He and Muhammad chuckled, but Moses remained steadfast in his seriousness.

"I cannot find humor when there are unfathomable horrors being committed all around us," Moses remarked. "Our religions, my brothers, are each so beautiful, and preach the benevolence of God, yet each have been used as instruments for destruction." He bit his lip, clenched his staff tightly and became silent. I could sense a great anger building inside.

"Go on my brother, Moses. Speak. The truth shall set you free," suggested Jesus. He patted him tenderly on the back. Moses let out a deep breath, and spoke.

"Five thousand years ago, I freed my people from the Pharaoh's persecution and led them from Egypt across the barren desert and back to Canaan." He turned to address me. "That's what you would call Palestine today, David." I nodded in appreciation for the clarification.

"On Mt Sinai," he continued, "God gave me the Ten Commandments so as to guide the conduct of the Hebrew people. We made a covenant and promised unwavering devotion to the will of God. But throughout the centuries that devotion has been desecrated and compromised, the vows constantly broken." He slammed his fist on the bar. "Look at what's happening in that area of the world today: murder, bombings, war, Jews killing Arabs, Arabs killing Jews, the cold blooded murder of innocent women and children. Is not one of the Ten Commandments, 'THOU SHALT NOT KILL?' How do they justify their murderous ways? Have they not yet figured out that violence begets violence? And that killing slays the seeds of peace? Do they not yet know that only Light can extinguish the darkness? That they should build bridges instead of destroy them? That they are all one people, connected to Source as well as to each other? When we kill another we also kill a part of ourselves."

With that he placed his elbows on the bar and lowered his head into his hands. Jesus and Muhammad consoled him. I felt helpless to soothe his misery. Nervously, I looked away, and my attention drifted to the television. I was glad the baseball game was still on. In a world suddenly surreal, where nothing seemed to make any sense, the game was the one thing that kept me somewhat grounded. The Yankees held a 2-0 lead over the Red Sox in the top of the fourth. Somehow, Pedro Martinez had evidently escaped the bottom of the second without further damage. Boston was now threatening with the bases loaded. However, there were already two outs and two strikes on the batter, Manny Ramirez. Hopefully, the Yankees would escape the inning with the lead intact.

Just then Moses raised his head and looked at the television. His mood seemingly changed from sadness to anger once more. Steadily he stood erect, his attention focused intently on the screen.

"And I'm sick of curses!" he proclaimed. "Just like my people, the beleaguered Red Sox have been the most cursed and persecuted franchise in baseball. They haven't won the World Series since 1918. Their fans suffer great humility and shame. I am tired of hearing 'The Curse of The Bambino.' My new motto is 'Reverse The Curse'!"

With that he thrust his arms high above his head. "Go Sox!" he boldly cheered. At that precise moment, the batter, Manny Ramirez, the American League's home run leader, took a mighty swing. The ball did not leave the park. Instead, it rolled softly up the middle. The Yankees' pitcher lowered his glove and appeared ready to snag the grounder and make the final out of the inning. But the ball rolled, untouched, through his legs. It continued its slow, deliberate path right up the middle towards second base. Both the shortstop and second baseman converged on the ball. I thought Derek Jeter would make the easy play. But as if the ball was divinely guided, it hit the bag and bounced high in the air, out of reach of the leaping infielders, and safely into the outfield for a base hit. Two runners scored. Bernie Williams, the Yankees center fielder, scooped the ball and unleashed a strong throw home. The ball sailed over the catcher's head and bounced into the seats. Another run scored. Unbelievably, the Red Sox now led 3-2.

"Yes!" screamed Moses, and for the first time a smile

appeared on his face. "So much for the so-called Curse of The Bambino!"

"Don't get your hopes too high, Mose. It's still early," remarked Muhammad.

I was bewildered by that wacky play. And more so by the fact that The Prophets really enjoyed baseball and took a rooting interest. I turned to Budd for clarification. He shrugged his soldiers.

"What can I say?" he offered. "They like baseball. It's a pleasant diversion."

Budd and I began a serious conversation. He pointed out that the world's three major monotheistic religions – Judaism, Christianity and Islam – are all very similar. All three believe in the notion of a single, true God, one who is powerful and eternal. All three revere the Ten Commandments as core precepts to their way of life. All three foster the notion of humanity's connection to something eternal, that all of Creation is somehow interconnected, and that meticulous, adult logic alone is not a sufficient tool to comprehend divine truths. And all three share the belief in the existence of angels as well as share common prophets. The Muslims believe the teachings of Moses and the message of Jesus, but not in his divinity. They believe the Jews made the mistake of denying the Mission of Christ, and that the Christians erred by exceeding the bounds of praise and deifying Christ. But again, he repeated, they are more similar than they are diverse.

As Budd spoke I thought of the irony: how all three religions were so similar, yet their followers so devoutly diverse; how religion is meant to unite, but instead all too often it divides. All three religions share common themes of grace, compassion and transcendent purpose. They influence, mirror, and support one another. And each refines concepts that reflect the same elemental truths. Yet, humanity was becoming perilously close to being extinguished by the divisive hatreds and violence of devout followers willing to kill and die for their beliefs. Moses was right: we need to build bridges, not destroy them.

I glanced at the Holy Ones. They were watching the baseball game with great interest. The Red Sox were now leading 7-2. They had blown the game open. It all started with that one incredible play, a seemingly benign grounder up the middle that should have been fielded for the final out. Then the next four batters all had base hits to chase the Yankees' starting pitcher from the game. Moses appeared quite content. Then, Jesus had a revelation.

"I think trouble is coming," he predicted.

"What is it?" asked Moses.

"Sniff the air. Can you smell that, Mose?"

Moses lifted his head and sniffed three times. On his third whiff he appeared to recognize a familiar scent. A look of concern crossed his face. He turned to Jesus.

"Smoke?"

"Yes, smoke."

"Oh Jesus, I can't catch a break," lamented Moses. "My earthly nemesis still torments me in the afterlife."

Just then the jukebox began playing a popular Eighties song, *Psycho Killer*, by the Talking Heads. I turned to the front door and saw the bearded being enter.

The Nemesis wasn't a prophet, nor a god.

And I had a feeling he wasn't one of The Advanced.

The only thing I knew for certain was that he was no longer of this world.

Chapter 4

THE NEMESIS SAT at a corner table, among the shadows, alone in the back of the bar. A waitress strolled by with an anticipated delivery, a pitcher of beer and a plate of hot nachos dripping with cheddar cheese, and placed them on the table before him. The Nemesis nodded in gratitude, though his gesture didn't look all that sincere. When she left, he filled a large mug with the golden libation and lit a rather large cigar. Behind him was a sign that read, "No Smoking", but he didn't heed its message. No one in the bar seemed to take offense. Or dared to challenge.

I had studied the doctrines of The Nemesis for two semesters in college. Judging by his appearance, the neatly trimmed gray beard and moustache, the carefully groomed hair, the custom-fitted white shirt and gray vest, I knew exactly who it was.

"Sigmund Freud?" I asked the genial stranger, Budd.

"The one and only," he replied.

"Why is he here? He's not a prophet."

"He brings a bit of comic relief to the Holy Ones with his deranged rants and ludicrous hypotheses. Sometimes, they play with him. Sometimes, he gets under their skin. Perhaps they enjoy the challenge."

Like Jesus, Muhammad and Moses, Freud's body had the same ethereal, translucent quality of the great religious icons who, to my continued amazement, were beside me in this very bar. However, noticeably missing from Sigmund Freud's presence was the blue-white aura that enveloped the three Holy Prophets. Already, I had a theory why.

"Does he know he's dead?" I asked Budd.

"No. He's still in denial."

Sigmund Freud looked admiringly at his full mug of beer, lifted it proudly like an elated baseball player who just robbed an opponent with a leaping catch at the outfield wall, and closed his eyes, bringing the glass to his eager mouth. He drank half at once. When he was finished, he placed the mug down on the table, and, as if making a bold statement, burped loudly before opening his eyes. Then he looked at us. His glance made me feel ill at ease.

"Why don't you all gather round my table for a drink," he said, and with a gesture of his arm he extended an invitation for us to join him. "Let's engage ourselves in a group discussion, shall we?"

"Oh boy," muttered Jesus under His breath.

"Here we go," mumbled Muhammad.

"If he starts in with me again I swear I'm going to clock him," proclaimed Moses.

With reluctance and a bit of trepidation, we rose from our seats and joined him at his table. The prophets seemed to be doing a poor job of concealing their unease. I had the feeling we were all passengers on a boat about to enter turbulent waters. I decided to make a pre-emptive attempt to steer the ship into calm seas.

"Is that a Cuban cigar?" I asked flatteringly, hoping to appease his ego while quelling tensions in a bid to initiate casual conversation.

He removed the cigar from his mouth, held it a foot or so from his face, leisurely rolled it with his fingers, studied the fine tobacco wrapping, then the label, and exhaled a large, satisfying cloud of noxious smoke that engulfed everyone sitting at the table.

"I don't know," he finally replied, a hint of pretentiousness in his voice. Then he looked directly at me and delivered a bold statement with a condescending tone. "Sometimes, a cigar is just a cigar."

I felt belittled. And I knew I could not hold my own against the master intellect in an academic debate. Thankfully, a prophet came to my aid.

"How are you doing tonight, Siggy?" asked Muhammad with a sigh. The prophets obviously had a nickname for every one on the other side.

"I am doing well," Freud smugly replied, and finished the rest of the beer in his mug. There was an uncomfortable silence as he reached for his pitcher and refilled his glass, not offering to share his beer with the others.

"I can't say the same for any of you," he added.

"What do you mean?" asked Moses, rather contentiously. I had a feeling the great Jewish prophet would be the first to challenge the master of psychology. Moses appeared eager for a war of words.

"First of all, let me start by acknowledging your greatness. A great man influences his fellow men in two ways: by his personality and by the ideas which he puts forward. You are all selfless, compassionate, benevolent beings. And you all preach common ideas of love, forgiveness, and, most importantly, faith to a single, eternal, almighty and omnipotent God who promises to care for his believers if they remain faithful to his worship. This grand notion strikes a primordial chord in every human being. You see, in the mass of mankind, there is a primal need for an authority figure that can be admired, before which one bows, by whom one is ruled, and, sadly, sometimes abused. The origin of this is a longing for the father felt by everyone from their childhood onwards, for the ideal we create in the innocence of our youth that our flawed father can never live up to. For the same father whom the hero of the legend eventually boasts he has overcome."

As Freud spoke I looked at Jesus. He rolled His eyes. Muhammad appeared to hear the words that were spoken, but I doubted he was truly listening. I could sense that he was bored. Moses nervously tapped his fingers, waiting for the intellectual analysis to stop, waiting for the proverbial 'but'.

"But," continued Freud, "you all have deep, psychological issues that need to be addressed. Each and every one of you."

"Well," said Jesus, "before you start attacking my brothers gathered before you, why don't you cast the first stones at me? I withstood the scorn of the angry mobs at the temple of Judea, the betrayal of Judas, the wrath of the merciless Pontius Pilate. Surely, I am strong enough to bear the brunt of your feeble insults."

"Jesus, ah Jesus," sighed Freud, shaking his head.

"Still at it, aren't you? Trying to be the Glorious Hero, the Great Savior of humanity. Trying to save all of your deranged friends gathered here tonight from what you misguidedly perceive to be venomous, therapeutic observations. Two thousand years later and The Messiah Complex is alive and well, I see."

"If it were in my power to save every soul in this world I would, regardless of the sacrifices needed."

"You really do have an inflated ego, Jesus, don't you? And you suffer from illusions of grandeur. Didn't you learn anything by dying on the cross? You cannot bear someone else's burdens. You cannot save someone else's misguided soul. You can only save yourself. It all starts with the individual. And in your case, I think you need to resolve some disturbing issues that fester deep in your subconscious. One, in particular, I suggest needs immediate attention."

"And what would that be, Siggy?"

"I think you have a Father Complex."

"Excuse me?"

"I said I believe you have a Father Complex. You were extremely angry at him when you were a young boy."

"That's absurd! I loved my Father. What on earth ever gave you the idea that I resented Him as a child?

"He abandoned you."

"Abandoned me?!?"

"Yes, abandoned you. He was never there for you, was he?"

"My Father is God! He was always there for me. Even today He is everywhere. His divine presence is in every one, in every creature, in every atom, in every thing, at every given moment."

"Come, come, Jesus. Get real," said Freud, tapping his cigar ash on the edge of the table before exhaling another cloud of noxious smoke and sending it flying in the air like a loaded missile in our direction. "Did he ever play catch with you in the backyard? Or help you with your homework? Or watch television with you in the family room on a Saturday night?"

"We didn't have a television."

"I see. So he neglected you, too?"

"Television had yet to be invented when I was growing up."

"A mere triviality."

Jesus remained patient, even though Sigmund Freud was not making convincing arguments. I couldn't tell if the psychologist was drunk or just sadly injudicious. Budd said earlier that sometimes the prophets liked to play with Freud, and sometimes he got under their skin. I wasn't sure what was happening now, if they were merely jostling with the cagey psychologist or if

Freud was actually getting the better of them. Budd was still sitting at the bar, his back to us, studying his glass of beer, so I decided to continue to silently observe the tête-à-tête.

Without warning, Moses slammed his drink on the table, and Sigmund quickly turned to face him.

"Siggy," demanded Moses, "back off! Leave my brother Jesus alone. Your arguments lack merit. They are preposterous. I'm so sick and tired of your inane psychoanalysis."

"Anger, Moses?" said Freud, in a voice that both belittled and antagonized. "After all these millennia you still haven't resolved that one fatally destructive aspect of your personality?"

"Man's iniquities to man are what truly stir my anger, Siggy. Not these pathetic arguments you make."

"Are you sure it's not some personal trauma, or dark, hidden psychosis which you repress that fuels your ire?"

"The only thing I'm repressing right now is my desire to crack you over the head with my staff!"

Freud shook his head as he poured another beer. Behind him, the photo of Classy Freddie Blassie once again caught my eye. Oh such irony, I thought. The pose Blassie was striking, arms outstretched like an angry bear, teeth clenched liked a madman, seemed fitting. It was as if the legendary wrestler wanted to leap out of the photo and strangle Freud himself, saving Moses the trouble.

"Do you know what I think, Moses?" continued Freud. "I believe you have a personality disorder. Technically, I believe you suffer from what I call 'Dual Personality Syndrome'."

"That's nothing but psychoanalytical gaga to me."

"Quite the contrary. I've studied the malady first hand. It is not, as you say, 'gaga'. And I've also done some extensive historical research on your life as well. It appears there was not one but two men named Moses at the time your religion was founded."

Moses looked confused. So was I. Attentively, we all listened to Freud's hypothesis.

"You see, the Jews possess a copious literature apart from the bible. In my research, I found that there was an Egyptian Moses, probably an aristocrat, whom the legend turned into a Jew, and there was also a Jewish Moses, the son-in-law of the Midianite priest Jethro, who was a poor shepherd keeping with his flocks when he supposedly received the summons from God. This Moses never traveled to the famed mountain in the Sinai Peninsula. Instead, he began preaching in a certain locality known as Meribah-Kadesh, a desert oasis in a stretch of country south of Palestine."

"What's your point?" asked Moses.

"I want to know which Moses are you? Or do you claim to be both?"

"What does it matter?"

"If you claim to be both, surely you are delusional. One cannot be two people at once and in two places at the same time. If, on the other hand, you maintain you were the Egyptian Moses, leading the Hebrews to the Promised Land, I think your people deserve to know your little hidden secret."

"What secret?"

"That you really weren't, 'one of them'."

"I was one of them in spirit, one in belief, united by a common cause, bound by a common dream. That's the heart of the matter. Besides, Jesus was a Jew and he gave rise to Christianity. What does it matter if I was Egyptian and helped found Judaism?"

Freud was silent for a moment, apparently lost for an intellectual retort. No one spoke. In the silence of unease, I glanced at the television. To my delight, the Yankees were chipping away at the big Red Sox lead, attempting a slight comeback. The score was now 7-5 in the bottom of the sixth and the great Pedro Martinez was walking off the field, being replaced by an unheralded middle reliever, much to the delight of the cheering crowd in the zoo known as the Bronx. I didn't have the heart to give Moses an update. But the prophet was starting to make his own comeback of sorts with Sigmund Freud. Soon, the analytical master regained his composure.

"That's a compelling argument. I'll give you a temporary reprise there," said Freud. Then he spoke with fullness of conviction. "But there is no denying the fact that you are a pathological liar!" There was obvious aggression in his voice.

"Pathological liar?" protested Moses.

"Yes!"

"I most certainly am not!"

"Yes you are!"

"No I'm not!"

"Yes you are!"

"No I'm not!"

They sounded like two pre-school kids arguing in a kindergarten playground. I couldn't help but chuckle at the silliness of their repartee.

"Face it Moses, you lied," Freud insisted.

"As God is my witness, I did not."

There was silence for a moment, but the expression on Freud's face spoke volumes. He slowly grinned, and I could feel the tension mount. It was as if he was a prosecuting attorney who just trapped the guilty defendant in a blatant lie in front of everybody on the witness stand. I think Moses sensed this, too. He slowly backed up in his chair. His breathing slowed and his shoulders drooped.

"What about the Ten Commandments?" he asked.

"What about them, Siggy?" Moses said with a snicker.

"Did God write them…or did you?"

"God did, of course!" he replied, rather meekly. Then Moses flinched. It appeared he was concealing something.

Freud smiled. His mind seemed to race. He was like a shark sniffing the first whiff of blood. He continued the interrogation with bold assuredness.

"Look me straight in the eye when you answer this question, Moses. Now I'll ask it one more time: did God write the Ten Commandments? Or were they scribed into stone with the very flesh and bones of your own mortal hands?"

This time Moses paused before answering. He started to get even angrier. His face turned beet red. He bit his lip hard. For a moment, I thought he was going to punch Freud. Then he released a deep, long breath and looked away, defeated.

"Answer the question Moses," insisted Freud. Everyone at the table was captivated by the unfolding drama.

"I wrote them," Moses softly admitted with resignation.

"Say that again, please, for all to hear."

"I wrote them!" Moses declared as he pounded his fist on the table. "But it was God's word that I transcribed in the stone. My hands were merely his tools."

"You admit you physically carved the Commandments in stone, don't you?"

"Yes."

"So, that explains why you were atop Mount Sinai – if you are the Moses of Egypt, that is – for ten long days. Or was it two weeks?"

"I don't remember exactly. It was a long time ago."

"You lied to your people, Moses! You lied to the world! Don't you feel horrible guilt?"

Moses looked distraught. His glow faded. His shoulders were slumped and his head seemed heavy atop his body. Then he took a deep breath and seemed to regain his strength.

"I didn't lie, Siggy. Your argument is all semantics. The Commandments really did come from God. Like my younger brothers, Jesus and Muhammad, God spoke through us so that man could understand His divine message. But it is His Word we spoke, not ours. Those were His words I carved into stone, not mine."

Freud started to chuckle. He seemed satisfied to

have made what he thought was an irrefutable point. It was obvious that his arguments didn't hold water. Deep down, I sensed The Others knew this, too. They easily could have ripped his dissertation to pieces. But for some unknown reason they didn't.

"Why do you torture me so, Siggy? You crucified me in your book, *Moses and Monotheism*. And still it continues today. Can't you let it rest? Just let it go. You need to move on."

"Don't turn the tables and assume the role of therapist with me, Moses. I am not the patient here."

"Life isn't black and white, Siggy," said Moses. "It's all gray, different shades of gray. But your mind is so calcified by logic and reason, littered with countless textbooks of clinical tests and psychological jargon, that I guess you simply can't understand. You have to let go, Siggy. Trust me. When you let go, you gain everything."

Freud poured the last remaining beer from the pitcher into his glass and looked at Moses with a sparkling gleam of victory in his eye.

"I'm afraid it's you who needs to let go, Moses. Let go of denial. Accept your malady."

"I am not inflicted with any sort of malady."

"Indeed you are. You need intense therapy. What do you say you see me for a one-hour session three days a week? You're a friend. I'll charge you the fair rate of $100 per visit."

"One hundred bucks? That's outrageous!" protested Moses.

"You should help your fellow man for free," interjected Jesus, "lest one day you need help from another."

"Do not desire for yourself what you also wouldn't desire for your neighbor," added Muhammad.

Freud laughed, then turned to confront Muhammad.

"Don't get me started with you, Mo. We could be here all night."

"Just bring it, brother," challenged Muhammad.

"You, my dear friend, also have some serious psychological disorders."

"Name one."

"For starters, you show all the classic symptoms of schizophrenia. And I know for a fact you harbor suicidal tendencies. I believe you have a 'Death Wish'."

"A Death Wish?"

"Yes."

"What are you talking about, Siggy?"

"I've taken the liberty to dig into your background, too. Seems you didn't, 'get the calling', until you were forty years old."

"That's true."

"While you were sitting all alone in a cave."

"That's true, too."

"Isolating oneself, being in solitude, is a common tendency displayed by nearly all schizophrenics," declared Freud.

"When we sit in silence, and still the mind, we can hear the voice of God speak to us," countered Muhammad.

"I think the voices you were hearing were the psychotic ones inside your head!" shouted Freud. "Did not the people of your time call you a madman when you first preached the word?'

"They did," he answered. "I will not deny that. But that was because they were wholly ignorant of the message I tried to preach."

"And were not there many attempts on your life by all the Arab tribes who saw you as a threat to their decadent ways?"

"Yes. They were angry because they refused to submit to the will of Allah and disavow their evil ways and their worship of idolatry. I challenged their way of life."

"So let's recap: time and time again, by word and by action, you knowingly placed yourself in harm's way?"

"I did what Allah asked me to do."

"Were you not offered untold riches by the many Arab tribes at the time to stop preaching?"

"Yes."

"Riches, I might add, that could have made you one of the wealthiest men alive and afforded you a comfortable, stress-free life?"

"Yes. But although they gave me the sun in my right hand and the moon in my left to turn my back on my undertaking, I would not pause until the Lord carried His cause to victory. Or until I died for it."

"Don't you see your Death Wish? It's quite evident."

"It wasn't a Death Wish. My wish was a Life Wish, for my people to live in a way that was reverent to all of earth's living creatures, a way honorable to Allah."

Again, Freud took a deliberate and dramatic pause. He puffed slowly and satisfyingly on his cigar. My eyes were starting to water from the smoke.

"Tell us all the story of Du'thur," Freud asked after the long delay.

Muhammad's eyes widened. His aura momentarily dimmed. Obviously, he was taken back at the mere mention of the name.

"How do you know about Du'thur?" asked Muhammad.

"As I said, I did my research," Freud proudly replied. "Thoroughly and exhaustively, I might add." He leaned back in his chair and twirled the remaining beer in his glass, as if he was a cultured Englishman sipping an expensive glass of port. Then he finished it and burped.

"One day, I was sleeping under a palm tree," Muhammad recounted. "Suddenly, I awoke to find an enemy named Du'thur standing over me. In his hand was a sword drawn and pointed at my chest. 'O Muhammad, who is there to save thee?' he callously teased. 'God,' I answered. Then, while attempting to strike, he stumbled and dropped his sword. I seized it, pointed it at him, and asked, 'O Du'thur, who is there now to save thee?' He looked at me with sad, defeated eyes. 'No one,' he said with somber voice and lowered his head, resigned to his fate. 'Then learn to be merciful,' I said, and handed him back his sword."

"SEE!" screamed Freud, spitting beer from his mouth and pointing his arm at Muhammad with great exclamation. "Muhammad has a suicide wish! Can't all of you at this table see that? An enemy tries to kill him with a sword, fails miserably, and Muhammad hands the sword right back to his enemy. Basically, he's saying, 'Kill me! Please, kill me! Oops, you failed once? No worries. Here's your sword. Try again'!"

"That enemy became one of my firmest followers," protested Muhammad. "You see, I gave him life when death was staring at his soul. That day he learned to be merciful."

Just then, the song, *Smells Like Teen Spirit* by Nirvana began playing. I suddenly had the suspicion that each time the music grabbed my attention, a Holy One would appear. It was as if, whether for drama, theatrics, or just heavenly fun, the gods all had their own entrance song when they arrived.

I turned to face the door. Sure enough, the Great Sage, the Awakened One, the man who attained Nirvana while still of earthly body and mind, walked in.

Chapter 5

IF HE WAS dressed like a monk in a baggy brown robe, tweed rope belt and wooden sandals, I would understand. Even a white toga would have seemed more appropriate, easy to accept. Instead, The Enlightened One walked in from the chill of the Wyoming night dressed like a gaudy American tourist making his first visit to Honolulu.

He was wearing Bermuda shorts and an unbuttoned yellow Hawaiian shirt, revealing a portly belly which he made no obvious attempt to hide. On his shirt was a bounty of colorful patterns: green coconut trees, brown pineapples, tropical birds in a whirlwind of vivid colors, and dancing hula girls with hair of red, blonde and brown. Concealing what appeared to be a bald or cleanly-shaven head was a straw hat. He wasn't wearing shoes, but covering his feet were long white tube socks pulled high to his knees.

Slowly, he waddled through the bar like a mellowed penguin, rubbing his belly with his right hand, seemingly proud of the protrusion, as if it were a badge of honor or a definitive physical proof of enlightenment. A large grin stretched from ear to ear, suggesting he was happy and at peace. He strolled past us without acknowledgement, slid out a chair, used it to prop himself atop the table behind us, then sat and crossed his legs. His back was to us and he faced directly into the wall. He began meditating.

"He looks like the maitre d' at Trader Vic's," snickered Freud. "Now there is someone who has completely lost touch."

"I beg to differ," I said with confidence. "I believe the Buddha would say just the opposite." I studied Buddhism only briefly in college, but still I felt my words were backed with assurance.

Sigmund Freud turned to me with a scowling look on his face. "Don't argue with me, young man. You are new here."

I thought Freud was about to launch a vicious diatribe at me. The Holy Ones chuckled, sensing my unease. Thankfully, Freud turned his attention back to

Buddha. He studied his subject for a minute or so, rolling his cigar ever so softly in his right hand, then rose from his chair and approached him.

"This should be entertaining!" said Jesus after he left.

Freud rolled his sleeves up as he approached Buddha, like a vigilant detective ready to interrogate a suspect in the holding cell at police headquarters. Then he sat down in a chair against the wall, opposite Buddha, directly in the Enlightened One's line of vision. Buddha opened his eyes. He neither smirked nor smiled.

"Good evening, Siddhartha," said Freud. "Or do you prefer I call you Mr. Gautama?"

"Yes," replied Buddha in a calm, gentle voice.

"Mr. Gautama? Or Siddhartha?"

"Yes."

"Well, which do you prefer?" Freud continued.

"I have no preference," answered Buddha.

For a moment, Freud seemed befuddled. Then with a sternness of voice he continued his query.

"I would like to have a serious talk with you. May I start by offering to buy you a drink?"

"I desire nothing, I refuse nothing."

Freud scrutinized Buddha's attire.

"Judging by your ridiculous outfit, may I suggest a tropical Mai Tai?" Then laminating his words with a snide veneer and delivering them with a condescending enunciation, he added, "with a little, pretty umbrella in it, too?"

"I desire nothing. I refuse nothing," Buddha repeated.

Freud snapped his fingers loudly to get the waitress' attention. When she came to their table he ordered a pitcher of beer for himself and a Mai Tai for Buddha.

"Extra rum!" added Buddha, as he discretely sneaked a wink at Jesus.

I was surprised by his acceptance of Sigmund Freud's offer of an alcoholic beverage. In my studies, I learned that Buddhist monks adhere to a strict regimen of discipline. They do not indulge in any forms of entertainment that can be viewed as secular. They eat only at appointed times. And drinking alcoholic beverages was not permitted. Nor were the use of any forms of intoxicants for that matter.

"Do not judge," said Jesus. "Tonight, haven't you witnessed that all is not as it seems?"

"He's just playing with Siggy, anyway," Muhammad informed me with a knowing smile.

"God, I wish I had Buddy's tolerance," lamented Moses, shaking his head. "That Crazy Quack always gets under my skin."

"Perhaps you would do well then to meditate,

Mose, or study the Buddha's doctrines," suggested Jesus. "They are quite remarkable."

"They most certainly are," agreed Muhammad. "I think his followers are onto something, that peaceful lot. Amazing how they have spread the beliefs of their religion with overwhelming pacifism. Islam spread through large-scale military conquest; Christianity has spurred innumerous wars of violence and bloodshed; acts of hatred and violence between Hindus and Muslims have plagued India for centuries. Somehow, the Buddha's great spiritual message has spread peacefully and without bloodshed."

The words Muhammad spoke echoed in my head. Religion and Peace: they seem always to be at odds. From my brief studies of Buddhism I remembered that its teachings of divine love and transcendent purpose were translated into a benign pacifism that impacted humanity on a very large scale. Indeed, pacifism and nonviolence were both characteristic of countries where Buddhism flourished.

Freud sat straight up in his seat when the waitress returned with the beverages. He blew a cloud of smoke in Buddha's direction. The Enlightened One didn't seem to mind. Freud took a gulp of beer directly from his pitcher, then began his interrogation.

"I have done some extensive research on you as

well, Siddhartha. There are some questions I would like to ask. Please, for your own good, give me honest answers. The truth will set you free."

"Truth is good," replied Buddha.

"Is it not true that you were born the son of a powerful and wealthy ruler of a small kingdom?"

"It is true."

"And that your father afforded you a life of supreme luxury, living as a monarch with three beautiful palaces, wearing clothes made of only the finest silks, dining on exquisite food and drink, being serenaded by music that was played by only the most beautiful of women?"

"It is all true."

"Then why did you rebel against him, refuse all he had given, and run away from home?"

"I didn't run."

"Be honest, Siddhartha."

"I am honest. I didn't run."

"You didn't run?"

"No. I walked."

Freud pounded his fist on the table. "Don't get smart with me, Hula Boy!"

"I walked away because the luxurious life I was afforded was an empty and useless existence. It was all illusory. The lifestyle offered no solution to the problem of human suffering. So, I walked, and found the path. The path to Awareness. The path to Non-Attachment. The path to Non-Self. I let go of my identity."

"So, you have an identity crisis?"

"Not at all."

"Answer me this: how do you see yourself?"

"I cannot attach a label to it."

"Why not?"

"Labels are meaningless."

"Work with me, Siddhartha. I'm trying to help."

"Well, in words you might understand, perhaps you can classify me as the 'Anti-Freud'."

Freud seemed offended by Buddha's choice of words. "The 'Anti-Freud'?" he asked. "Explain, you heretic!"

"I have released any notion of Ego. I have tamed the Id. Therefore, I have no use for the Superego. Hence, I found Enlightenment."

"Ah yes, enlightenment. Speaking of which, is it true that you found so-called 'enlightenment' while sitting on a straw mat beneath a Bodhi tree atop a mountaintop in western India?"

"That is true."

"After seven days of not eating or drinking?"

"That, too, is true."

"Did it ever occur to you that your so-called 'enlightenment' might actually have been a grand hallucination, a vision of delirium, produced by the body's adverse reaction to extreme dehydration and food deprivation?"

"That is not true."

"How do you know?"

"I am Enlightened. I know."

With that comment, Buddha smiled ever so gently at his interrogator. He raised his glass and began sipping loudly through a straw. I sensed that Freud was getting frustrated. Nothing the cagey psychologist said could apparently disrupt the blissful state of the Enlightened One. Then, Jesus rose and approached Freud.

"Why don't you take a momentary break from the questioning, Siggy," said Jesus. "Come indulge me in a friendly game of pool."

"I am not interested in playing games, Jesus!" declared Freud. "I am trying to enlighten you all as to the underlying psychological traumas and deep-rooted psychosis that may have contributed to your feelings of omnipotence and created all those so-called 'divine experiences'!"

"Perhaps we can put a friendly wager on the game?" Jesus calmly insisted.

With that Freud's anger seemed to subside and his eyes filled with delight. It was as if he, too, found enlightenment or some deep epiphany to a once ambiguous psychoanalytical hypothesis.

"Jesus a gambler? You devil you!" he said with glee in his voice. "You're on!"

"Loser buys the next round?"

"Deal – but no funny stuff, Jesus. I don't want to see any miracle shots or impossible comebacks."

"I thought you didn't believe in my divinity, Siggy."

"I don't. Nonetheless, I want to make it clear that any form of chicanery will not be tolerated."

Everyone except Buddha rose and headed to the pool table on the other side of the room. Instead, he resumed his meditation on the table. As we strolled through the crowd, no one seemed to notice the presence of the Divine Ones, or Sigmund Freud for that matter. Instead, the eyes of the strangers only made contact with me. I felt an uncomfortable sensation that I was out of place, like a corporate executive wearing pajamas to a board meeting, or an innocent kid playing on the wrong side of the tracks. Then I remembered that Budd had said that most people were incapable of seeing the true essence of the Holy Ones, oblivious to the divine presence that was all around the bar. Evidently, I was the one who stood out.

The pool table closest to the juke box was open. Muhammad racked the balls tightly as Jesus chalked his cue. Freud observed the remaining three pool sticks carefully, then selected the biggest one. He held it proudly, like an expensive cigar, and rolled it with his hands before chalking it. He had a smirk of confidence etched on his face. I was hoping Jesus would beat him, and beat him handily.

"I used to be quite adept at billiards," Freud proudly proclaimed.

"I know," said Jesus.

"Go ahead then," he said smugly. "I'll let you break."

Jesus gracefully walked to the head of the pool table and placed the cue ball on its appropriate mark. With elegance, he lowered his body and lined his shot, rocking the stick back and forth three times in his hands with a slow, gentle motion. As he cocked the stick all the way back for the break, the light overhead flickered dramatically like a flash of lightning. Finally, he unleashed a powerful shot, and as stick met ball a thunderous impact echoed through the bar. The colorful balls scattered from the violent collision in different directions, each dropping one by one into the six different pockets of the pool table. All the while, the cue ball danced amidst the colorful frenzy of stripes and solids, banking off the padded sides, forming first one triangle and then another on the green felt surface. I felt a sudden sense of wonderment when I recognized the pattern as the sacred Hebrew Star of David. Moses smiled. Muhammad subtly pumped his fist in glee. Soon, the white ball was the only one left on the table. Every ball had been sunk on the break!

"Liar! Cheat!" screamed Freud. "That's not fair! I refuse to accept defeat."

"Defeat?" asked Jesus. "I'm afraid you are wrong. It appears you are the victor here."

Jesus pointed to the pool table. My eyes followed. The cue ball was still rolling, ever so slowly, but rolling still, inch by inch, in what seemed like a steady, unending procession, until it fell with a quiet thud into a side pocket. It was a scratch. Jesus had made a miraculous shot, and lost.

"WHOOOOOO!" screamed Freud with glee, and he fell to the floor shouting, flailing his arms and kicking his legs into the air like a lassoed bull in a Mexican arena in the most unsightly of victory celebrations. "I win! I win! I win!" he proclaimed.

Jesus looked at me and grinned.

"I did that for you, David" he confided.

"Why? I was hoping you would win."

"I know. But I wanted to prove a point. Look at him. You just had the thought he looked like a lassoed bull in a Mexican arena. To be more accurate, I would say he looks like a jack ass!"

I laughed. Hearing Jesus' choice of words was something I didn't expect.

"Think about it, David. He did nothing to 'win' that game. He didn't even attempt a single shot. Right now, he is taking delight in someone else's misfortune. Do not gloat when your enemy fails; when he stumbles, do not let your heart rejoice. Those that do not heed these words all look like jack asses to us in the spirit world."

I looked at Freud, still beside himself with glee, as he stood and raised his arms in the air, proclaiming his greatness.

"Learn to be humble" continued Jesus. "Everyone who exalts himself will eventually be humbled, and he who humbles himself will be exalted."

He turned to me. "Besides, was that not a spectacular shot?" He asked in a tone that was not bragging.

"Yes, it was."

"Might I be bold enough to say, 'miraculous'?"

"Yes. But you still lost. The cue ball went in the hole."

"Would that shot have been any more incredible had the cue ball not fallen into the hole?"

I thought about that. Fifteen balls all were sunk on

the break. And the cue ball traced the diagram of the sacred Jewish symbol in the process. I would give anything to have the talent to execute a shot as unbelievable as that. So, too, would all the great pool players of the world.

"No, I guess not," I realized.

"Losing does not diminish the magnificence of that shot. Did I lose the goodness of and purity of my mission when I was persecuted and nailed to the cross? The message I spoke, the actions I undertook, still echo through eternity because their essence was comprised of truth and beauty. My physical death couldn't diminish their power, just as the cue ball falling in the hole at the very end cannot lessen the magnificence of all that happened on that pool table. Labeling something a win or a loss, judging something good or bad, diminishes the action and tarnishes its beauty. Do not judge or you too will be judged. For in the same way you judge others, you will be judged, and with the measure you use, it will be measured to you. As you walk your path in life, be a bright beacon for those who need your light to see. Be a healer, not a critic; a light, not a judge."

The words resounded in my head, the lesson sunk into my soul. They echoed for a long time deep in the core of my being.

"Now, can I interest you in a game of darts?" Jesus offered.

"I wouldn't stand a chance against you!" I exclaimed.

"Come on, David. I'll play left-handed."

"I don't think so."

"In all seriousness, I believe you should go spend a little time with Buddha. He's done meditating."

I turned to look at the Enlightened One. He was still sitting upright on the table, his legs crossed, facing the wall. And he was as still as a statue. It didn't even appear as though he were breathing. I was certain he was still in a deep meditative trance. But who was I to argue with Jesus.

"How can you tell he's not meditating anymore?" I asked.

"He finished his drink," Jesus noted. "Plus, I saw him making eyes at that pretty waitress you find attractive."

"He did?"

"Gotcha! Gotcha good!" laughed Jesus, again sounding like a geek. "But I am serious when I say he would welcome your company. It's why he's here."

It's why he's here. Those words echoed in my head. Was he here for me? I wasn't sure if that is what Jesus meant. In truth, I wasn't sure of a lot that was happening tonight. But I was determined to find out. Doing as Jesus suggested, I left The Others at the pool table and walked back to the corner of the bar where Buddha was sitting. As I approached, he turned and smiled ever so softly. I could sense the peaceful state that enveloped him.

"Hi, I am David," I said making my introduction.

"I know," he replied.

"Of course you do. I'm sorry."

"You are forgiven."

My eyes were unintentionally drawn to his bright, yellow shirt, replete with all the hideous tropical patterns of flora and flying birds and fish. And the comment made by Sigmund Freud, comparing Buddha's attire to that of a waiter at the Polynesian restaurant, Trader Vic's, popped into my mind. I couldn't help but chuckle, silently, to myself.

"I believe his exact choice of words was maitre d', not waiter," corrected Buddha, who, like the others, was evidently able to read my thoughts.

"With all due respect, may I ask why you are dressed like that?"

"When in Wyoming, do as the Wyomans do," he replied matter of factly.

"But they don't dress like that in Wyoming," I informed him.

"How was I supposed to know? This is my first time here."

Slowly, he uncrossed his legs and began to rise. It seemed to require great effort on his part. I heard his joints crack, saw the grimace on his face, and with sincere empathy felt the apparent weakness of his muscles and the pain in his bones.

"I'm not as young as I used to be," he lamented, with great resignation. Then he leaped high into the air, executed a stunning double summersault, segued into a graceful spinning twist, and landed perfectly, like an Olympic gymnast, on the hardwood floor. I was astonished!

"Gotcha! Gotcha good!" he said with a gentle laugh. "Jesus taught me to have a sense of humor, bless his soul."

He patted me affectionately on the shoulder, and once again I could tell he was speaking in serious tones.

"Anyway, if truth be told, I dressed like this for Sigmund. I knew it would get under his skin."

"Why are you guys tormenting him?" I asked curiously.

"We are not tormenting him. We are helping him. Even though he has passed to the spirit side, he still clings tightly to earthly illusions. His eyes are open, you might say, but still he does not see.

"And really, David," he continued, "it doesn't matter how I am dressed. What is physical appearance, but what the mind determines it to be? This hat, these garments, even my portly belly which you noticed earlier, are mere illusions. The mind is everything. What you think, you become. All that is, is the result of what we have thought."

I was having a difficult time fully digesting the wisdom of his words. Buddha seemed to sense my confusion.

"Let's take a walk outside," he suggested. "There's something I want you to see."

We walked outside into the cold October night. The temperature felt as though it dipped well below freezing. My teeth immediately began chattering and I rubbed my arms for warmth. Buddha, dressed in shorts and a Hawaiian shirt, didn't seem to be affected by the cold at all. I looked at his attire and was amused at the thought he seemed dressed for a Caribbean island rather than the cold mountains of Wyoming. Then I began to envision that I, too, was on a warm, tropical beach. I could picture my feet in the hot sand, feel the warm breeze gently caress my face, imagine the bright sun infuse my entire body with warmth and light, hear the sounds of the waves on the ocean and children's laughter upon the wind and the loving crash of surf when sand was kissed by the sea. Soon, my teeth stopped chattering. I was no longer bothered by the chill of the night.

"Bet you're not laughing at my outfit anymore," he quipped.

"Not anymore," I happily confirmed.

"Good. You are starting to understand."

He raised his head high and gazed at the night's sky. "Look up to the heavens," he suggested, "at the billions of stars and galaxies in the universe. What do you see?"

I looked upwards to the sky but I couldn't see a single star. An ominous cover of clouds rolled in quietly during the time I arrived in Lander, concealing the celestial lights above.

"There are no stars. I see only clouds," I said.

"The clouds are the veil of illusion. They prevent you from seeing the stars. But not seeing them does not mean they are not there. Surely, they shine brightly, if only you could see beyond the illusion."

He paused momentarily, waiting to be sure I understood. Then he continued.

"And I will tell you that nothing is permanent. No form endures forever. The sky above is constantly changing. The clouds, sooner or later, shall pass, revealing to your eyes the lights of the heavens. Furthermore, nothing exists independently or externally. Everything is connected with One. The clouds are part of the sky, the sky part of the earth, the earth part of the cosmos. You and I are both standing here on the pavement, in some place called Wyoming, connected to earth and therefore to the sky, and therefore to the infinite cosmos as well. We are One with all."

Buddha walked a few feet away to a large oak tree on the corner. He reached high to the nearest limb and plucked a leaf from the branch. Then he turned and showed it to me.

"What is this?" he asked, raising it with his right hand into the light of the street lamp that illuminated the darkness between us.

"An oak leaf," I answered.

"A oak *leaf*, you say?"

"Yes. An oak leaf."

Then he raised his left hand to the leaf and, holding it firmly in his right, ripped it all the way to its stem.

"What is it now?" he asked.

"An oak leaf *with a tear*," I answered, trying to be precise with my observations.

"*A leaf with a tear*. Is that your new label?"

"Yes."

"Is it no longer whole?"

"Not anymore. You ripped it."

"And is it still not part of the tree?"

"No. You pulled it from its branch."

"I would argue that the term 'oak leaf' is misleading. This is still part of the tree, is it not? And is it not part of our being, too? You see, the leaf of a tree, if examined closely, is simply a transitory collection of processes. The lines dividing the smallest possible components of the oak leaf from you and I are imposed by our own perceptions. They do not actually separate that transitory leaf of the tree from anything. The line between 'an oak leaf' and 'not an oak leaf' is an illusory one. That's why one should never take labels to seriously."

I was having trouble fully comprehending the wisdom of the lesson he was trying to impart. Again Buddha sensed my puzzlement.

"Knowledge is communicable," he said tenderly, "but wisdom is not. And words do not express thoughts very well. They always become a little different, a little distorted, once expressed in speech or written on paper. That is why what is of value and wisdom to one man often seems foolish to another."

"Yes," I agreed, feeling as though I grasped at least one profound insight. In my rush of knowing, I attempted to communicate some wisdom of my own.

"Just like God. Words cannot even begin to describe God's divine magnificence. God is not bound by physical or temporal limitations. God is beyond definition. And God is beyond the human intellect's ability to fully comprehend."

"Very good. You understand more than you know." He patted me reassuringly on the shoulder, like a father acknowledging a lesson mastered by his son. "You must be feeling a bit overwhelmed by all that is happening tonight. There is a lot to understand. And I am not here to give you a detailed description on the doctrines of Buddhism. For now, let me give you a few simple axioms that might linger productively in your consciousness: We are what we think. All that we are arises with our thoughts. With our thoughts we make the world. Anger, ignorance and selfish desire are our greatest enemies. Avoid what is evil. Do what is good. Practice loving friendship, compassion, altruistic joy and equanimity. When you see someone practicing the Way of Giving, aid him joyously and you will receive great blessings. Those are just some of the universal truths of life."

"Thank you," I said. "I understand them all."

"Good. Now let's go back inside. I'm freezing my butt off out here in these shorts!"

I laughed at his remark. Irony, it seemed, was a

prevalent commodity this evening. And I admired his refreshing lack of concern over how he appeared and how others perceived his appearance.

"By the way," he said, "that was not an oak leaf."

"Oh, no?" I said, with a tinge of both sarcasm and joy. "What was it then? An apple? A coconut? Or perhaps a twenty dollar bill? After all, they say money grows on trees!" I laughed at my clever response. Buddha, however, remained serious and sincere.

"If truth be told, it was the leaf of a cottonwood tree. Oaks don't grow in Wyoming," he informed.

We walked back inside the bar and the atmosphere seemed livelier than when we left. Muhammad was playing pool with Sigmund, and based on the way he was gloating I believe the master psychologist was winning. Moses watched despondently in the corner while Buddha went back to his table and resumed his meditation. I walked to an empty bar stool between where Jesus and Budd sat. The Ike and Tina Turner classic, *Proud Mary*, was now playing. I wondered if another God was making an appearance.

"No," said Jesus. "I just played this song in honor of my blessed mother and my dearly beloved wife," He proudly confided.

His words grabbed my full attention. "Wife? You were married?" I asked. He became a bit reticent.

"I prefer not to talk about my personal life," He confessed.

"Are you ashamed?"

"Not at all. Most of my life reads like an open book anyway, no pun intended. It is her privacy I am concerned with."

"Tell me, please."

"Later," He said.

My head was spinning like a furious tornado. I was still attempting to process all that Buddha had told me. And now Jesus dropped a bombshell. I had read several theories that insisted Jesus was married to Mary Magdalene, and that they had a child, a daughter named Sarah. Hearing the innuendo on His part seemed to confirm that as well as the question of His divinity. According to the most popular theories, Mary Magdalene was not a prostitute but descendant of royal blood. When the current bible was compiled around 325 AD, over eighty gospels chronicling the life of Jesus were in circulation. Almost all spoke of Jesus mortality and his marriage to Mary. They regarded Him as a holy prophet, an enlightened being, but a mortal man nonetheless. All but four were destroyed. The ones the Church of Rome retained when they adopted Christianity as the empire's new religion – Matthew, Mark, Luke and John – were greatly embellished, making Jesus a deity, not a man, and His word above reproach. At least that's the way the conspiracy goes. I wasn't sure which was true. But Jesus being a man, an enlightened one, yes, but a man nonetheless, made the most sense to me.

"Nothing is as it seems," He said. "And everybody loves a conspiracy. Don't believe all that you read."

I nodded.

"Now, do you want me to tell you about my wife?" He asked.

"Yes. Please."

"Can't."

"Why not?"

"I was never married!" He poked my sides and laughed. "Gotcha! Gotcha good!"

Again, my head was spinning. In an attempt to still the relentless musings for a brief moment, I glanced at the television. The Red Sox were still leading the Yankees 7-5 in the top of the ninth. Surprisingly, I wasn't all that disappointed. In light of everything unfolding tonight, the game didn't quite have the same significance as it did earlier. I wondered if baseball ever would again. Still, it was a welcome diversion and once more gave me a sense of normalcy in a very abnormal time.

I watched the game for a few minutes without engaging anyone. Even Budd sat quietly without interrupting my solitude. Then the sounds of another unusual song swayed my consciousness, one with a distinct Middle Eastern flare.

"He's here," said Budd.

"Who?" I wondered.

"See for yourself."

I turned toward the door and saw him. My philosophical mentor. My Spiritual Guru. The One who's writings I cherished and whose timeless wisdom I revered. The One who had made such a profound impact on my life.

The Arabic music now made perfect sense.

The Prophet from Lebanon was in Lander.

Chapter 6

WITH LITTLE FANFARE, save for the Arabic music that greeted his entrance, The Prophet walked unceremoniously into the tavern. No one paid heed to his arrival. Even the Holy Ones seemed not to notice, nor did he acknowledge their presence. Quietly, he took a seat in an open area near the middle of the bar.

The Prophet wore a gray sports jacket and light blue shirt unbuttoned at the collar. From a pocket lining the interior of his jacket, he retrieved a pack of Camel cigarettes, tapped them on the corner of the bar, pulled one out and lit it with a wooden match. Soon the bartender welcomed him, and he ordered a cup of coffee and a double shot of arak, a Middle Eastern liquor.

To millions of twentieth-century Arabs, this poet,

artist and philosopher, born in Lebanon, a land that produced many prophets, was revered as a local genius of his age. But Kahlil Gibran was a man whose art and inspiration spread far beyond the Middle East. He was a truly gifted writer. No author impacted me as much with his provocative thoughts and rhythmic syntax of words. His short stories and poems always read like a beautiful melody, profound words accompanied by powerful chords, serenading the reader with their immense ability to lighten, elevate and uplift. His classic masterpiece, *The Prophet*, written nearly a century ago, is still the most widely-quoted book at wedding celebrations today.

Sitting alone in the shadows of the bar, his demeanor looked far from uplifting. His body was ethereal and he was embraced by the same blue-white aura as The Holy Ones, but his mood seemed down, distant and perhaps even distraught.

"That's because he's seduced by The Muse," said Budd.

"The Muse?" I asked.

"Yes. He's working on a new book, *THE IMMOR-TAL BEYOND*. The writing process, I hear, can be both exhilarating and exhausting."

After a few minutes I excused myself and headed to where The Prophet sat. I was not going to let this opportunity pass without having asked Gibran some profound questions, hopefully receiving some great insight in return.

"Hello Mr. Gibran," I said, extending my hand. "I'm sure you already know my name." One thing I discovered this evening was that all the Holy Ones knew my name even before I was formally introduced.

He looked at me with dubious eyes. A skeptical smirk became etched on his face. My first thought was that I offended him.

"Know your name?" he asked, contentiously. "What do you think I am? A warlock, or witch doctor, or sorcerer?"

"I'm sorry," I said, apologetically. "My name is David."

"I know!" he declared, erupting in laughter. "Gotcha! Gotcha good!" He, too, sounded a bit silly when he said those words. "Jesus the Comedian has been a great inspiration on my life. We both agree a sense of humor is truly a sense of proportion."

"Yes, Jesus does believe in the healing power of laughter."

"'He that is merry of heart hath a continual feast'," quoted Kahlil, in a tone reminiscent of his writings.

"Did you write that?" I asked.

His expression turned quite serious, almost angry, as if I had falsely accused him of some egregious crime.

"No. Proverbs 15:15. I would never plagiarize. Especially not the bible."

He took a sip of coffee, then chased the hot beverage with a cool swig of arak.

"What brings you here?" I asked.

"The drama," he said. "It's great theater, is it not?"

"It certainly is. Totally unbelievable. My head is still whirling by all who have appeared tonight. Including you."

Once again he seemed a little agitated.

"I meant the baseball game," he informed, pointing to the television.

I understood all of Gibran's writings and gained great inspiration from his philosophy. At this moment, however, meeting the great poet in person, I seemed to be misunderstanding the simple things he was saying. I seemed to be on the express while he was riding the local.

"I'm a little superstitious," Gibran confessed. "I was watching the game at home and my lucky chair didn't seem to be working. I felt the need to come here in hopes of changing the Yankees' fortunes"

I looked at the television. The Yankees were now trailing 8-5 in the bottom of the ninth. It was their last chance to pull out a come-from-behind victory. There was one out and a runner on first. With the seeming inevitability of defeat close to becoming reality, I was a disheartened for the first time. The enthusiasm felt during twenty-five years of being an avid fan doesn't get diminished in one night, even if it is an evening spent with great spirits from the beyond. For the moment, I shifted my focus away from the Holy Ones. I was watching my beloved Yankees. I was hoping their season would not end tonight.

"Don't worry," said Gibran. "If one more guy gets on base, Derek Jeter will come to the plate representing the tying run for the Yankees. It only seems fitting. He's having an outstanding game. Have you been watching?"

"A little bit, here and there. I've been distracted."

"He's got three hits and four of the Yankees' five RBIs. Been quite spectacular in the field, too. His glove has saved at least two runs."

We watched in silence as the drama continued to unfold on a baseball field more than two thousand miles away. Kahlil's attention was acutely focused on the screen, as was mine. The Red Sox decided to make a pitching change. The network went to a commercial break. With the drama put on hold for a few minutes, I saw an opportunity to engage him in thought.

"Is Jesus the Son of God, or a mortal man?" There it was. I dropped the big one right off the bat. I wanted to get straight to the point and knew I only had a couple of minutes before the game resumed.

He took a drag off his cigarette, thought silently for a moment, blew the smoke into the air, and turned to me with deep knowing in his eyes.

"I know of one truth," he said.

"What is it?" I asked.

"It is simple, yet complex."

"I am ready to listen."

"Before I tell you, behold here is a paradox: the deep and the high are nearer to one another than the mid-level to either. If you desire divine insight, and truly want to understand the great truth I speak of, you must first sit beside a river in the valley of your yearning and gaze with wonder upon a tiny rock."

I was perplexed. "I don't understand," I said.

"In other words, start by asking a few simpler questions. You know the common adage, 'walk before you run'."

I didn't know why, but I felt he was purposely being coy and evasive. Attempting to redirect my plan of attack, I panned the room, searching for a new strategy. The picture of Classy Freddie Blassie again caught my eye. Once more I was reminded of the sadness felt on the day he died. Deep down, I always believed in the eternal nature of life and felt that death was nothing more than a doorway to another enchanting world. Now, I wanted confirmation from a spirit who was not named Jesus, Muhammad, Moses or Buddha, one who hadn't founded his own religion.

"Tell me of death," I asked The Prophet.

"A funeral among men is a wedding feast among the angels," he said. That was it. Short and succinct. He spoke no more. Instead, he took another drag off his cigarette, rolled his tongue around the inside of his mouth, and blew smoke rings into the air. I continued to probe.

"Is death a reality of life?" I posed.

"The reality of Life is Life itself, whose beginning is not in the womb, and whose ending is not in the grave. For the years that pass are naught but a moment in eternal life, and the world of matter and all in it is but a dream compared to the awakening which we call the terror of Death."

Those words resonated in my soul like some deep, universal truth. Then I realized why: The Prophet was quoting his own immortal words from *The Prophet*. The proverbial flood gates were now opened as he continued to speak with minimal prodding.

"For what is it to die but to stand naked in the wind

and melt into the sun?" he continued. "And what is it to cease breathing but to free the breath from its restless tides that it may rise and expand and seek God unencumbered?"

He appeared to be in some sort of trance as he spoke those words with a beautiful, melodic cadence. I decided to continue a query in a style similar to *The Prophet*, hoping to keep him in this state of mind before repeating the question of Jesus' divinity.

"What of prayer?" I asked, just as the priests did in his literary masterpiece.

"People pray in their distress and in their need. Why not also pray in the fullness of one's joy and in one's days of abundance?"

"And what of religion?"

"Is not religion all deeds and all reflection? Who can separate his faith from his actions, or his belief from his occupations? Your daily life is your temple and your religion. Whenever you enter into it take with you your all. He to whom worshipping is a window, to open but also to shut, has not yet visited the house of his soul whose windows are from dawn to dawn."

"And of God?"

"If you would know of God be not therefore a solver of riddles. Rather, look about you and you shall see Him playing with your children. And look into space;

you shall see Him walking in the cloud, outstretching His arms and descending in the lightning and the rain. You shall see Him smiling in flowers, then rising and waving His hands in trees."

He spoke of God. Now, surely, he was ready to divulge the secrets of the Son of God.

"And what of Jesus?"

"What about Jesus?" he asked, turning to face me, his voice no longer rhythmic and trance-like.

"Is he really the Son of God?"

"I can't answer that right now."

"Why not?" I asked.

"The ballgame is back on."

I was disappointed. The great wordsmith was on a roll, enumerating verse after verse from his classic writings. I thought I was close to receiving the elusive answer. But, without warning, the narration abruptly stopped. I knew in my heart he was merely avoiding the question.

His attention turned back to the television. Reluctantly, so did mine. I would have preferred the answer to my question first, but I was determined to get it when the game was over.

Keith Foulke, the ace closer for the Red Sox, was now on the mound. He was nearly unhittable. Boston was two outs away from victory, poised to bury The

Curse of The Bambino in dramatic fashion, right in the very House That Ruth Built. The situation looked dire for the Yankees.

To my surprise, Foulke walked the first batter he faced on four straight pitches. Either he was extremely nervous or the Curse of The Bambino was again working its magic.

"Enough with The Curse!" commanded Moses. Like cats, both he and Muhammad stealthily appeared and now stood right beside us watching the drama unfold. I looked for Jesus. He was playing darts with Sigmund Freud and, judging by Freud's bitter reactions, he was winning.

Kahlil's baseball prophecy came true. Derek Jeter, the Yankees captain and inspirational leader, now stepped into the batter's box representing the tying run. The Yankee Stadium crowd was in a frenzy, imploring their hero to perform a minor miracle.

"Come on Jeets!" cheered Muhammad, caught up in the moment.

"He's going to hit it out of the park," predicted Kahlil.

"End it now!" pleaded Moses. I couldn't help but get swept wholly into the drama as well.

The first pitch Derek Jeter saw was a slider. It was low and outside for Ball One. The second was a fastball that sailed high. The count was now 2-0. Surely, Jeter would get a good pitch to hit. Foulke delivered a fastball. Jeter got exactly what he was looking for. He swung and swung mightily, driving the ball deep into the night before it landed in the right-centerfield bleachers. The game was tied!

"Damn that Curse!" Moses yelled in bitter disappointment as Muhammad, Kahlil and I all cheered in delight. The moment was beyond surreal. Not only did Derek Jeter hit a dramatic home run to tie the game, not only were the Holy Prophets appearing before me tonight in a strange bar in Wyoming, but they were also deeply caught up in the excitement of a baseball game, too.

The inning was not over. Gary Sheffield, the very next batter, the Yankees' Most Valuable Player during the regular season, lined a triple down the left field line on the very next pitch from Foulke. The Stadium crowd was delirious. Now, a slow ground ball or a deep fly could win the game. A base hit was not necessary for the Yankees to be victorious.

Jorge Posada stepped to the plate. With only one out the Red Sox brought their infield in. Foulke looked at the catcher, Jason Varitek, for the sign. When he had it, he got into the set position. First, he checked the runner at third. Then he delivered another blazing fastball. Posada swung and lined a scorcher down the line. But the Yankee magic, for the moment, would end right there. The third baseman caught the line drive and immediately stepped on the bag for an unusual inning-ending double play. The game was headed for extra innings. Moses seemed relieved. Muhammad, Kahlil and I were grateful the game was tied but disappointed that the Yankees were so close to winning and came up short.

"Strange," remarked Kahlil, "the desire for certain pleasures is part of my pain."

With another commercial break filling the airwaves, I resumed my query with Kahlil. I wanted an answer to the question that had been passionately debated by humanity for the past two millennia.

"What about Jesus?" I asked.

"Once every hundred years Jesus of Nazareth meets Jesus of the Christian in a garden in the hills of Lebanon. And they talk long; and each time, Jesus of Nazareth tells Jesus of the Christian, "My friend, I feel we shall never, never agree."

"I don't understand."

"Jesus is often misunderstood."

"Yes, He told me. But is He Divine?"

"There are three miracles of our brother Jesus not yet recorded in the Book: the first that He was a man like you and me; the second that He had a sense of humor; and the third that He knew He was a conqueror though conquered."

"You said He was 'a man like you and me'. So He was a mortal after all?"

"I didn't exactly say that," Kahlil remarked, shaking his head. Then he pointed to a small crucifix that was behind the bar, partially concealed between the cash register and a bottle of Jamaican rum.

"What do Christians see when they look at a crucifix?" he asked.

I studied it for a moment. "They see a man dying on the cross for the sins of mankind," I answered.

"Yes. And they see a man in great agony, suffering as he clings to life, do they not?"

"I would assume most do."

"And every year on Good Friday, the anniversary of His death, humanity honors Him with funeral orations, lamentations, and weeping. Perhaps humanity would do well to see a great spirit wearing a crown of thorns, holding out His arms to the infinite and gazing through the veil of death into the depths of life, conquering death through death, and giving life to those who lie in their tombs."

"So, He is the Son of God?" Again, I was unsure.

"I am merely saying that humanity all too often sees

in Jesus a man who was born poor, who lived like a wretch and was humiliated like a weakling, crucified as a criminal. I say Jesus did not live in poverty or fear; neither did He die suffering or complaining. But He lived in revolt, was crucified as a rebel and died a giant."

Kahlil was painting a picture of Jesus as a mortal man. Then once again he seemed to change his tune.

"As I was saying, Jesus did not come from beyond the blue horizon in order to make suffering a symbol of life, but rather to make life a symbol of truth and liberty. He did not come down from the supreme circle of light to destroy dwellings and build church steeples and monasteries over their ruins, nor to persuade men to become priests or pastors. He came to breathe into the air of this earth a spirit as powerful as it was new, with the strength to undermine the foundations of all the monarchies erected over the bones of mankind. He came to demolish the palaces constructed over the tombs of the weak and to destroy the idols erected over the corpses of the poor."

"So, He was the Son of God?"

"Jesus did not come to teach men how to build huge cathedrals and opulent temples alongside humble cottages and cold, dark hovels. He came to make the heart of man a temple, his soul into an altar, and his spirit into a priest."

"Was He God or man?" I insisted.

Kahlil sighed. "You won't let it go, will you?"

"No, I won't."

"As I said earlier, I know of only one great truth."

"What is that one great truth?"

Kahlil took a long, purposeful drag of his cigarette, and followed it with a sip of drink. Then he looked directly in my eyes for a few seconds, as if trying to make sure I was fully ready to comprehend the depths of the words he was about to speak. When he finally spoke, it was with authority and conviction.

"If what Jesus preached was beautiful and true, does it matter whether He was God or man?"

I was stunned by the profoundness of the reply. He repeated it again to make sure I fully grasped its essence.

"Really, if what Jesus preached was good and came from a Higher Source, does it matter whether He was God or man?"

Kahlil was absolutely right. Jesus spoke of Love and Truth. He inspired millions to live a better life. Isn't that all that matters? And maybe it's a more compelling story if He *was* a man who attained god-like acumen while on this earth as opposed to a God who became imprisoned in flesh and blood. Still, I didn't have an answer to the age-old question. Just then I looked across the bar where Jesus was standing with The Others. He smiled at me and winked, as if He knew the question of His true divinity, for this moment, still remained a mystery.

"I must be going," Kahlil said, rising.

"So soon?"

"Yes. I can't focus on this game with all your incessant questioning."

"I'll stop asking questions until the game's over. I promise!"

He smiled. I knew he was only teasing.

"Actually, I don't want to worry my wife," he confessed, "I told her I was just going out for a pack of cigarettes and it's been over an hour."

"You have a wife on this side of life?"

He chuckled. "Half of what I say is meaningless. I say it so that the other half may reach you."

We shook hands. He wished me luck on my journey, and reminded to always remain humble and to keep a fertile and open mind. Then, quoting *The Prophet* one last time, he left me with three lines of wisdom.

"Only when you drink from the river of silence shall you indeed sing. And when you reach the mountain top, then you shall begin to climb. And when the earth shall claim your limbs, then shall you truly dance."

With that he turned to go, a skip in his step and a little jitterbug shuffle on his way out the door.

I returned to my original seat in the front corner of the bar. Budd was still there. The game was now into extra innings. Both realizations comforted me. I ordered a beer and offered to buy him one as a well, but he declined. He informed me that he only consumed one drink whenever he went out. I looked at his bottle of Heineken. Amazingly, it was still half full, even though I had witnessed him take countless sips throughout the night.

Then from the jukebox came a haunting sound, the raspy voice of Johnny Cash from the very last album he ever recorded. The song was, *And The Man Comes Around*. The music was prefaced by an ominous verse from the bible, spoken by Cash, with his withered, crackling voice.

"And I heard as it were, the noise of thunder," the verse warned.

In the distance outside, I, too, heard the faint rumble of thunder approach.

"And one of the four beasts said, 'come and see', and I saw," Cash continued.

The Holy Ones humbly took seats beside Budd and

me at the bar. They seemed somber, apprehensive, as if a dark prophecy was about to become reality. Budd was quiet, too. For the first time all night, I noticed everyone else in the bar – the ones who weren't aware of the divine beings among them – were aware of something else.

"Trouble is coming," Jesus remarked with foreboding tongue.

"And I beheld a white horse…" finished Cash.

The strumming of the acoustic guitar began. The sound of thunder outside increased, getting louder and louder as the bar got quieter, soon drowning out the music with its frightful, deafening roar. And then I realized the ominous sound didn't emanate from the heavens. Rather, it was produced from the intoxicating power of hundreds of horses that guzzled high-octane gasoline for fuel and often carried wicked men with evil intentions.

Something bad was about to happen. I could feel it in my bones.

I looked at Jesus, Muhammad, Moses and Buddha. And what I saw scared me.

All at once, their auras grew dim.

Chapter 7

THE DEAFENING ROAR ceased with suddenness, but the air of inevitable doom did not. Evil, it seemed, was not only tapping at the threshold, but ready to kick the damn door in without knocking.

"And one of the beasts said, 'Come and see', and I saw," continued Cash, the music ending, the portentous biblical verse continuing.

"And beheld a pale horse, and the name it said on it was Death. And wherever he went, Hell followed."

The song ended. My heart sank. The bar was transfixed by some pending, dreaded event. Fear made its presence known in the faces and the breathing and the silence of the patrons. Even the gods were mum. Then came the sound of heavy boots on wood, and, as the

front door slammed open, the unholiest of trios saun-
tered in.

They walked slowly and with purpose, three bikers from hell dressed in black leather, wearing black
frowns, carrying black intentions. A cold, unforgiving
darkness seemed to hover over their heads and perme-
ate the entire bar. The leader was a behemoth of a man,
at least three hundred pounds, hair covering his face
and arms, a human grizzly bear hungry for trouble. To
his side was a muscular brute wearing a black leather
vest that revealed massive tattooed arms, a tattooed
neck, and even the ink-stained dome of his shaved
head. And the third beast was a tall, toothless warrior
with scars on his face and a long black ponytail that
looked as slimy and menacing as a snake. They walked
with fists clenched, and I could see their fingers were
adorned with shiny metal rings that bore skulls and
crossbones and other symbols of darkness and death.

They walked toward the far side of the bar where
the three Native Americans quietly sat, and approached
them with a brewing rage and contempt. I wasn't sure
if they knew them as some sort of rival gang, perhaps
even had a violent history with them, or if the three
bikers just had blind prejudice as their guide.

"I like red necks," were the first words spoken by
the man-bear of a leader to the Native Americans, "but

I hate red skins." He spat tobacco juice on the floor in front of them.

The biggest of the Native Americans raised his glass and downed his shot of tequila in a seeming show of defiance.

"We mean no trouble," the biggest of the Native Americans said in a voice that was neither inflammatory nor threatening.

"We kicked your red asses off this land a hundred years ago," said the bald-headed brute with an unmistakable reverberation of hate in his voice.

"You better leave now, or we'll be fixing to do it again," warned the tall, pony-tailed thug.

The three Native Americans rose simultaneously from their seats. The biggest of the three, the very same one who downed his shot, stood face to face with the leader of the unholy trinity, their bodies separated by inches. He was at least as big as the man-bear biker, perhaps even larger, and he did not look intimidated at all. For what seemed like an eternity, but was probably only ten seconds, he stared him down with pride in his face, matching wills and returning the same menacing stare. I thought a bloody, violent confrontation was inevitable.

"We were on our way out before you came," he

said. Slowly, the three Native Americans buttoned their jackets and headed for the door.

"Chicken shits!" screamed the snake-haired thug as they walked away.

The Native Americans stopped dead in their tracks. With their backs to the bikers, they clenched their fists. The restless silence warned of violence. We all held our collective breaths. The leader sighed deeply, then relaxed his hands. He motioned for his friends to ignore the insults and continue their path to the door. With that, the Native Americans departed peacefully and without incident.

"I need some whiskey," said the man-bear biker. "Bartender, get us some whiskey down here!" he demanded.

"It's last call," she said. "We're closing." I had the feeling she was lying, hoping the unholy trio would leave.

"Closing? I don't think so. Get us some whiskey."

"Sorry, I said last call." She tried to sound stern, but the crackle in her voice revealed her unease.

The behemoth of a beast grabbed her left arm and forcefully pulled her slender body into the bar. No one came to her aid.

"I'll tell you when it's last call, bitch!"

That was all I could stand. Whether emblazoned by

beer or feeling empowered by the events of the evening, I leaped out of my seat and confronted the man-bear. I wasn't afraid. After all, I had the gods on my side.

"Let her go!" I demanded as I stood before him, my shoulders arched back, my fists clenched and an expression of fearlessness on my face to prove my resolve.

The behemoth man-bear looked down at me in disbelief. Then a smile opened on his face and I saw missing teeth and tobacco-stained gums and smelt the rancid stench of beef jerky and cheap liquor and burgeoning wickedness on his breath. Slowly, he released his left hand from the bartender's arm and, with a stealthness of motion, grabbed my throat with his right. It was a powerful embrace. Instantly the air was choked out of me, my confidence gone with the wind. I was frightened beyond belief. With slow deliberation he raised me, cackling like a demon about to commandeer an innocent soul, until my feet were at least a foot off the ground. I struggled to release myself from his powerful grip but to no avail. 'Help me Jesus', I prayed in silence, unable to mutter a word. 'Now, someone, now'! I had a sickening feeling in the pit of my stomach. Something was about to happen, and I knew it wasn't good.

"So, you want to be a hero, hey boy?" exclaimed the behemoth of a biker. His cohorts cackled like demons along with him. Then with his free hand he unleashed a punch to my stomach that was so hard I swore I was hit by a wrecking ball. It felt as though life was literally knocked out of me. He released me from his evil clutch and I staggered to stay on my feet. Then he hit me in the face with a roundhouse punch that was delivered with all the impact of a rumbling locomotive. I felt a tooth fly out of my mouth as my body crumpled help-lessly to the hard wooden floor.

"Help!" I heard the bartender scream. "Jay! Mo! Help him!" she pleaded. "I thought you were his friends!" But there would be no help coming from the Holy Ones.

"I have always preached to turn the other cheek," remarked Jesus.

"Violence only begets violence," said Muhammad.

"Alas, I am too old and too weary to fight," lament-ed Moses.

"I am a man of peace, a lover of tranquility," de-clared Buddha. "Besides, this must be happening for a reason. Everything does. And I don't want to mess with karma."

"You are all a bunch of cowards!" Sigmund Freud scolded the gods. "And you call yourselves prophets and saviors? No wonder attendance is down in your temples and churches! People are losing faith in your religions and turning to all that New Age garbage for guidance!"

"Why don't *you* help him, Siggy?" I heard one of the Holy Ones say.

"I can't. They have obvious anger-management issues. That makes them prospective clients. I don't want to jeopardize any potential doctor/patient trust."

The beating continued while I lay defenseless on the floor. Instinctively, I rolled my injured body into a fetal position and covered my face as the unholy trio began kicking me with their hard, steel-tip boots. The sounds I now heard were a cacophony of boots hitting wood and steel-toed leather smashing my flesh. Every blow was delivered with incalculable power, my body being dented, battered, bruised and broken. I noticed a pool of warm, fresh blood widen and grow under my face. Surely, I was going to die.

Just then I heard a thunderous crash and a shattering of glass, as if a lightning bolt had demolished the front window. The beating abruptly stopped. And in the aftermath of thousands of shards of glass landing on wood, and the gasps of dozens of surprised people, resonated a booming commandment that sounded like the voice of God.

"GET YOUR FILTHY PAWS OFF HIM YOU BUNCH OF NO-GOOD PENCIL NECK GEEKS!"

With all my effort I raised my head slightly from the ground, and with eyes blurred from blood and tears beheld a heavenly vision. Here in Lander, coming to my rescue, dressed in skimpy blue wrestling tights with a world championship belt around his waist, was my savior, Classy Freddie Blassie!

"Look at this crazy old quack in a bathing suit!" remarked the beastly man-bear of a leader.

"If you're looking for the swimming pool, it's down the road you old loon!" said the bald-headed tattooed beast.

"And I think Elvis is there, too," added the demon with slimy black snake-like hair. "You can give him back that ugly belt you borrowed from him." With that the unholy trio laughed a devilish roar.

Fast as lightning, Freddie Blassie charged the behemoth man-bear and knocked him onto the pool table with a thunderous wrestling clothesline maneuver. The table broke upon impact, collapsing to the ground like a flimsy house of cards, as colorful pool balls raced along the floor in all directions. The bald-headed brute took a big swing at Freddie Blassie, but missed. The wrestling legend ducked another vicious hook, locked the thug's shoulder with one arm, grabbed his groin with the other, and lifted him high above his head, his arms and legs flailing helplessly in Blassie's grasp. Then Blassie sent him crashing to the ground with a devastating body slam that broke the thug's spirit and surely some of his bones. The biker with the long snake-like ponytail stared unblinking in disbelief at this white-haired wrestler who was faster than a lion and stronger than a bear. Freddie smiled, then kicked him hard in the stomach, cinched a headlock on him as bent over in pain, and sent him crashing head first into the floor with a beautifully executed wrestling move called a DDT. Freddie rose to his feet, but the unholy trio did not. The battle was over in seconds. Everyone in the bar roared with delight.

The man-bear slowly raised his head. He saw the carnage caused by the old man, the devastation of his gang, tasted his own blood upon his lips, felt the unwelcome embrace of defeat all around him, and heard the enthusiastic applause of the appreciative patrons in the bar.

"Who are you?" he asked the white-haired avenger in a voice that sounded as though it carried both wonder and fear.

"Tiger Woods you asshole! Now get the hell out of here before I take my three-iron and shove it up your ass!"

The leader crawled with obvious pain to his fallen buddies and began to shake their listless bodies. When his accomplices finally regained consciousness, the three bikers staggered to their feet, then hurried from the bar. The thunderous roar of Harley Davidson engines was once again heard as they started their bikes, but this time the sound no longer felt ominous. Instead, it seemed more like a loud scream of defeat, a deafening plea for pity, a tormented wail as the motorcycles raced out of town, away from the danger of this godsend, back to the lonely, comfortable safety of their lost dreams, their dark wishes and their wretchedness.

"Are you hurt bad kid?" asked Blassie as he leaned over my battered body.

"Freddie, is that really you?" I asked with a voice that was weak and raspy.

"In the flesh!" He paused for a moment. "Well, sort of."

I tried to raise a hand to touch him but could not. The pain was debilitating.

"I think they broke my ribs," I said with garbled speech. "And I'm missing a tooth."

"Can you stand?"

"I don't think so."

Freddie bent over, raised my fallen body, and carried me like a fireman to a booth with a padded seat. I was in excruciating pain, barely able to stay conscious. My clothes were ripped and bloodied. I knew I needed medical assistance.

"My face is numb. How bad does it look?"

"Like fresh hamburger meat. And your nose is the size of a zucchini. But don't worry: help is on the way."

"Did you call an ambulance?"

"Two, in fact," said Freddie, pointing over his shoulder before taking a step backward to let Jesus and Muhammad approach. I wasn't exactly happy to see them at this particular moment. Besides my body, my feelings were also hurt. I felt as though they had abandoned me in a desperate time of need.

"Why didn't you help, Jesus? Why did you forsake me?"

There was a look of guilt and concern on the Holy One's face. He knelt beside me, slowly surveying the damage to my eyes, mouth, cheeks and forehead. Then His grin turned to a gentle smile.

"I didn't forsake you, David. You didn't need my help…until now."

With that His aura grew bright and intense. I squinted, nearly blinded by His light. He reached His hands to me and softly cradled my battered face in His palms. I felt the healing hands of love, compassion and kindness. And then a miracle began to unfold. My face got drier, the wounds began to heal and close, the swelling subside. His smile widened and He leaned forward and kissed the gash on my forehead. The wound closed, and silently I laughed at the thought that this was the "Anti-Moses Kiss", closing instead of opening, mending the river of blood as opposed to separating the Red Sea. Soon, all sense of pain and injury was gone.

"All better now," He said.

Then Muhammad gently placed his hands atop my head and closed his eyes. My mind instantly became clear and alert. My spirit felt strong and expansive. It was as if, moments ago, I had been a deflated balloon. Now he was filling my entire being with energy, light and warmth, a beautiful air infused with enthusiasm and bliss. Energized and empowered, I couldn't help but smile.

"Good as new," he proclaimed, removing his energy-infusing hands from my head.

"Look," said Moses, holding a mirror before me. To my delight, my face was completely healed. There was no blood, nor scabs, nor signs of scars. I was elated. Even the missing tooth was back!

"I'm proud of you," said Moses. "Your intentions were noble, even if your hopes were a bit too ambitious."

Buddha approached. "That was a gracious gesture. You deserve a gift." He removed the straw hat from his head and placed it upon mine.

"Thanks, but no thanks," I replied.

"Why not?"

"No offense, but I think it's ugly."

"It is beautiful."

"Not to me."

"And it is precious."

"Precious? I'm sure I can buy one of these at the corner gift shop for two bucks."

"It is precious because it is a gift, David. All gifts are precious and should be received humbly, with grace and gratitude."

I felt ashamed. Buddha was absolutely right.

"I'm sorry," I said. "Thank you very much."

"You are welcome very much."

When he left I took the hat off my head and placed it on the chair beside me. Just because it was a gift didn't mean I had to wear it. I knew I could give it to someone who might appreciate it more than me.

Again Jesus kneeled and looked me straight in the eye.

"Do you want to know the real reason I didn't join the fight?" He asked.

I knew the answer. Countless priests recite the line

at church and I heard his voice repeat it during the attack. "Because you always taught us to turn the other cheek," I replied.

"True, but that's not all. You see, when I watched you approach those rabble rousers, I had a grand vision." Jesus looked upward toward the heavens, His imagination now in a faraway land. "I saw you as a mighty warrior, like the great Maximus Decimus Meridius himself, Commander of the Armies of the North, General of the Felix Legions, loyal servant to the true emperor of Rome, Marcus Aurelius, the general who became a slave, the slave who became a gladiator, the gladiator who defied an emperor, a fearless warrior in the venerable coliseum, defeating every formidable challenger who ever had the misfortune of fighting him. At the time, I really thought you were going to kick all three of their evil asses."

"Really?" What a fantastic compliment, I thought.

"No. Gotcha! Gotcha good!" He laughed heartily and poked my side with His finger.

"OUCH!" I screamed with fierce agony as His finger pressed my side. "My ribs, they're still broken!"

"Oops, sorry, I forgot about them." Then Jesus gently placed His hands on my ribs. Within seconds I could feel the bones fuse together, the ligaments once again tighten, the internal throbbing stop. The healing process was complete.

"You can stand now," He said. "There are others here who want to greet you before they go."

"Others?"

"Yes. Some of 'The Advanced'. Stand and see for yourself."

I rose and noticed a small group of spirits had gathered around the table, all recognizable historic celebrities who were deceased, or should I say living on the other side of our comprehensible realm. They were lined in a procession, ethereal bodies all enveloped by an aura of light, and one by one they greeted me with grace and reverence and bestowed some heavenly advice.

"There are two ways to live your life," said the great Albert Einstein, shaking my hand, his hair still wild and scraggly in the afterlife. "One way is to live as if nothing is a miracle. The other is to live as if everything is."

"Life is too important to be taken seriously," said the immortal Oscar Wilde, patting my shoulder. "Seriously, it is," he added.

"Life is either a daring adventure or it is nothing at all," said Helen Keller, no longer blind in this plane of existence. I was captivated by her beautiful eyes that sparkled in a vivid emerald and violet hue. She even winked at me.

"No person was ever honored for what he received," said President Calvin Coolidge. "Honor has been the reward for what he gave." With that he stood, proud and erect, and saluted me before leaving.

"Let us judge not, that we be not judged," said Abraham Lincoln, one President following the other. "I honestly know that to be true: it's how I got my nickname." Then Honest Abe winked before leaving, too.

"To be wronged is nothing unless you continue to remember it," said a white-haired Asian man who I assumed to be Confucius.

"I am," he confirmed.

Then came Benjamin Franklin. "Beer is proof that God loves us and wants us to have fun!" he proclaimed, holding two bottles of beer. He handed me one and clinked my bottle with his as a gesture of goodwill. "And remember: there cannot be good living where there is not good drinking!"

"Good works are links that form a chain of love," said Mother Teresa. This time I winked at her, grateful for the insight. She blushed.

"Be ashamed to die until you have won some victory for humanity," was the advice of Horace Mann.

"Never lose an opportunity of seeing anything that

is beautiful," intoned Ralph Waldo Emerson, clutching what seemed to be a book of new poems in his right hand. "Beauty is God's handwriting. It is a wayward sacrament, and thank God for it as a cup of blessing."

"Snakes don't wear vests because they have no arms," said Steven Wright.

I was startled by the comment as well as the presence of the comedian. Noticeably missing was a translucence of body and the discernable aura around his being. His appearance amongst The Others confused me.

"What are you doing here?" I asked the deadpan comic. "You're not dead."

"No, but my NFL football career is," he replied with straightness of face.

"You don't play football. You're a comedian."

"Exactly." He cracked the slightest of smiles. "Actually, I come here all the time. I have a summer cabin just outside of town."

"Can you see The Others, too?" I asked.

"The Others?" he asked. He looked around the room. "Just the usual crowd." Then he looked at me with concern on his face. "Don't get freaky on me, man." With that he left.

I looked around the room. The Others, who only moments ago were lined up to greet me, were gone.

But the Holy Ones were seated at the corner table with Sigmund Freud, and I saw Freud listen for the very first time, with what looked like total respect, and start to heed the sacred words of Jesus. Perhaps they were finally getting through to him, leading him to the Light. I continued to scan the bar. Budd was still in his corner seat, but hard as I tried I could not find Freddie. I dearly wanted one last chance to talk to him, tell him things I couldn't say when he was relinquishing life on his death bed, give him a super-sized thank you and a great big hug. Desperately, I searched the bar for the famous wrestler wearing skimpy tights in the cold of Wyoming, a friend who saved me from beyond.

"I'm over here, kid," he called out from the other side of the bar. "Come down and buy me a drink. It's the least you could do after I just saved your scrawny little ass!"

"I thought you didn't drink, Freddie? That's what you told me: never a drop in your life."

"That old life, maybe. But this is the afterlife, kid. There are different rules here."

As he requested, I ordered two shots of single malt whiskey and a couple of bottles of beer. He toasted me with his shot, downed it in one fast swoop, and chased the whiskey with an entire bottle of beer. He placed the empty bottle on the bar, then downed the second shot.

"Ah, that was good. Thanks kid."

He seemed quite happy and I was amazed at his physical appearance. Like The Others, he had an ethereal quality to his body and an obvious glow enveloped his being. And to my pleasant surprise he looked young, strong and vibrant, thirty or perhaps forty years younger than the last time I had seen him when he lay dying on his hospital bed.

"On this side of life, kid, one can appear any age. It all depends on the intentions of the beholder. You chose to see me as I appeared in that photo on the wall. Good choice. I do miss the sequin robes I used to wear to the ring, though. And it's pretty damn cold here in Wyoming. Maybe next time you can be a little more considerate!"

"But you wrestle best in tights," I jested. "Besides, I think your performance was just fine seeing the way you handled those tough guys."

"Still got it, hey kid?"

"Still got it."

Just then I had the sudden realization that although Freddie spared me, he used physical violence. I was confused. Violence always begets violence, I had been told. And he was now operating on a much higher spiritual plane. Was there no other way to save me than resort to physicality?

"Yes and no," he answered. "You see, every one eventually finds themselves on the path to the Light. Sometimes, however, a few misguided souls remain seduced by the darkness, not knowing the way out. On these very rare occasions, they sometimes need one of their guardian angels to give them a good old-fashioned kick in the butt to get them headed in the right direction."

"You mean to tell me you're their guardian angel?"

"Yours too, kid."

At that my eyes began to well. We had a long conversation about his life and the wisdom he rediscovered since his death. He informed me that once he crossed to the spirit side, all the fear he carried in life ceased to exist. He was consumed with love and reverence and forgave all those who had begrudged him as a mortal: the fans who threw eggs and spilled acid on him in the rowdy arenas; the prejudiced gangs that chased him at 100 mph on dark southern highways in the black of night, firing bullets at his car; his own children who had closed their lives to him; and all the women who had broken his heart in his youth. He was also deeply concerned for his three wives who were still living in the earthly world, all whom he betrayed and hurt. He hoped their pain had eased and that they had found forgiveness, too. Not because he wanted to be released of guilt – a human emotion, he said, that doesn't exist in the spirit world – but because he wanted their burdens to be lightened, their hearts opened, their spirits not to weighted by unnecessarily carrying hurt and sadness to their graves.

"Freddie, you seem so enlightened. We never had such profound, spiritual conversations when you were alive. Before, we only spoke of work, women and wrestling."

"That's because when I was alive I was sleeping. It wasn't until I died that I awoke."

We talked about what I had learned tonight. How death is a part of life, not the end of it. And how all of the world's major religions, though unique and diverse, speak of the same eternal truths.

"To quote the great Muhammad, 'Religions are like rivers, lakes, streams and oceans: all are different, yet all contain water'."

"Muhammad the Prophet?" I asked

"No, kid. Ali the boxer! The Greatest, as he likes to call himself. He has become quite profound in his latter years. Anyway, the point I'm trying to make is that one must see the truth in each, understand that all share some basic common tenets, and don't blindly accept one dogma as more righteous than the others. All have their merits; all are a path to spiritual awakening. But there are many paths, not just one. And the soul walks not one, but them all. Now, enough of this philosophical crap!"

With that he grabbed an unopened bottle of beer that was left on the bar and stuffed it in his tights.

"Gotta go now, kid. There are others who need my assistance. But don't worry: I'll always be watching your back."

He gave me a long, heartfelt hug. My eyes once again started to moisten. I was sad that he was leaving again, but glad to know that he still lived in another world, one greater than the one I knew, one beyond my ability to fully comprehend while living in an earthly body on this earthly plane.

"Goodbye you Old Bastard!"

"I love you, kid – even though you are a No Good Piece of Shit!"

With that he left, waving to the patrons who cheered as he passed. With a proud swagger, he walked right through the broken glass window from which he came, back to the beyond, back into the blackness of the cold Wyoming night.

Chapter 8

FOR THE FIRST time the jukebox was silent. I decided to play some songs. To my dismay, there was a sign that read, "Out of Order." How could that be? All night long I heard many songs play. Retrieving a quarter from my pocket, I decided to give it a try. No dice. I kicked the jukebox slightly, hoping to get my change back. The Rolling Stones classic, *Sympathy for the Devil,* began to play. I was gripped by fright. Panicked, I kicked the jukebox again. The song changed to, *What if God Was One of Us,* by Joan Osborne. Relieved, I decided not to test the hands of fate again. Joan Osborne would do just fine.

"Nice choice of songs," remarked Budd as I resumed my seat beside him.

"Still the same Heineken?" I asked.

"The same one."

Another unsolved mystery, though far from the biggest of the night. I ruminated on the evening's events, the appearance of the Holy Ones, my near-death experience with the bikers from hell, and my physical salvation that came in the form and spirit of my dear departed friend, Classy Freddie Blassie. I rubbed my jaw, amazed that it was healed, glad that I saw Freddie, grateful for the whooping he put on the evil ones.

"I feel sorry for those poor fellows," stated Budd.

His comment stunned me.

"Why?" I asked. "They came into the bar looking for trouble and nearly beat me to death. If anything, I am the one who should have been pitied when I lay defenseless and bloodied on the floor."

"No, I pity them."

"They nearly killed me! How can you pity them?"

He paused before answering.

"Our thinking is often inverted. All too often we look with sorrow on the victim and scorn the victimizer. But it is never the injured person who needs pity, rather the one who inflicted the injury. And whenever you forgive those who you fancy have hurt you, you are placing under each a stepping stone to a higher life."

As I reflected on his wisdom, I noticed that in the very corner table where Sigmund Freud grilled the Holy Ones, the master psychologist was still the attentive listener. As Jesus spoke, Freud closed his eyes. I believe he was trying to hear the soul of the message without being sidetracked by visual distractions. Soon, a slight aura appeared around his being for the first time. He must finally be grasping the message. Then he began to snore. I realized he had not been listening intently to the words of Jesus: he had merely fallen asleep! Still, Jesus continued to counsel him.

"When he sleeps, he truly hears the message," remarked Budd. "That is why he glows now. It is when he thinks he's awake that his mind still refuses to accept the Truth."

Budd obviously was a very profound man. All night long I had listened to him explain the bizarre happenings unfolding in the bar while getting a crash course on the history of the world's various religions. Not once did I ever decide to probe deeper into his background, his psyche. It seemed his waters ran deep, very deep, and that the man with the half bottle of Heineken was a wise soul indeed. And I still had no clue as to who he was.

"Are you a prophet?" I asked.

"Not really," was his response.

"A god?"

He chuckled. "I am no more a god than you are."

"Then who are you?"

"I am just Budd. Remember?"

"What are you?"

"You might say a messenger, a guardian."

His body wasn't translucent like The Others. At times I thought I saw an aura surround his being, but then it would quickly disappear. He definitely had the ability to read my mind, though.

"Are you of the earthly plane or the spiritual world?" I asked.

"I am of flesh and bone."

"Are you an alien?" I said half jokingly, but after the events of tonight I was ready to believe anything.

"No, but I have heard of other worlds where there are beings who were once just like us but have advanced well beyond our level. On those planets there are no wars, no crimes against each other. They are devoid of material ambition and the lust for power and possessions. They are utterly unselfish, living for the good of each other, in complete harmony with the universe. What a beautiful way to live."

I wasn't surprised to hear about life on other planets. There are billions of galaxies in the universe, each with billions of stars. It would be arrogant to believe earth was the only planet that contained life. How Budd knew about life on other planets didn't concern me. I took it as truth. More importantly, I was heartened to hear that the aliens didn't appear to be like the scary, evil sci-fi creatures of the Hollywood-hit movies, *Alien* and *Predator*.

"Mighty impressive-looking creatures, though," said Budd. "Those Hollywood special-effects wizards are quite imaginative."

"You seem enlightened."

"I possess knowing from beyond, of what once was and of what could be."

"Are you from the future?"

"In a manner of speaking."

"My future?" I don't know why I asked. I just felt this deep, inexplicable connection to him.

"It is difficult for me to explain, or for you to comprehend at this moment."

"Try me."

"Let's just say that time is not linear. It does not go from one point to another in a straight, continuous line. Rather, it is more spherical in nature."

"Spherical? That's a difficult concept to comprehend. We gauge our lives based on yesterday, today and tomorrow, always going forward, each day getting one day older."

"And hopefully, each day getting wiser."

"Hopefully," I said, "before too much time runs out."

"First of all, time is an illusion. It never runs out."

"How then is it spherical?"

"We will all best be able to understand it when we shift our perspectives. Let me give you an example of linear versus spherical thinking: one thousand years ago, every human being on this planet believed the earth was flat. Now imagine if someone back then had the capacity to travel across oceans and mountains and deserts. Say they began a journey due west, beginning right here at this very spot in Lander, Wyoming. Their journey would take them across the Rockies, the north Pacific, Japan, Asia, Europe, and so on. All this time, under the illusion the earth was flat, they would truly believe they were getting further and further away from this point of origin. Now if they never deviated from a straight line, eventually they would end up right back here in Lander, befuddled, confused, unable to explain how eventually their journey – going straight ahead all the time – brought them back here, full circle, right where they started."

"Yes, that would be inexplicable, giving their lack of perspective."

"All points in time are accessible at any given moment. We just cannot grasp that perspective yet, nor navigate ourselves within that realm. When we are ready, we will understand that on other dimensions one can amend the past just as easily as alter the future."

Change the future as well as the past? What a revolutionary concept. And he spoke of aliens. If tonight taught me one thing it was to be open-minded and not to judge. But had I not experienced the extraordinary events of this evening, and had a positive intuitive feeling about Budd, I might have labeled him a weirdo or a quack.

"Be careful with your thoughts," Budd remarked, obviously reading mine. "When you become one of The Advanced, you will realize that thoughts have the same power to heal or to harm as do actions and words."

"I'm sorry. I meant no harm when the word 'quack' popped in my head."

"I know. No apology is necessary. Besides, I am incapable of being hurt by another's judgmental remarks. It is the less evolved I am warning you about. They can still feel the power of your thoughts, even though they do not realize the source of that energy. It makes the less evolved become insecure, or worse, confrontational, like those three bikers who were here earlier."

"How does one evolve?"

"Through experience, which brings growth and change. They are vital while of body on this earth."

"I always believed change to be a good thing."

"It is. Change expands us. Anything which tends to harden our outlines is suicidal. We are petrifying when we hold onto anything that is either material or mental, especially after we get a glimpse of better things. One's mind, as well as one's heart, should be kept open, expansive, ready for revelation, able to see the next lesson God presents. That is how we evolve."

"Are we eternal?" I asked, seeking confirmation for my own beliefs.

"Yes. All humans are spirits only visiting this world. All spirits are everlasting beings. But the irony is that one must give one's life to keep it eternally. One must give all one has for the general good of each other, for it is in giving that we endure and grow. Jesus preached that we are our brother's keeper. His ultimate good should be our first thought and our last. To serve one's fellows is to build immortality. And to love one's neighbor as oneself, as all the major religions preach, is also a simple law of self-preservation. 'He who giveth shall receive tenfold; he who keepith for himself shall inevitably lose it all', including himself."

I thought of all my friends who were still caught in the rat race, working jobs that no longer brought satisfaction, justifying their sacrifice because of the size of their paychecks. They were seduced by money, the power it could provide, the material possessions it could bring, but deep down their hearts were sad and their souls were crying. It is unfortunate that so many cling tightly to their material possessions and perceive the accumulation of financial wealth as a means to attain happiness. The soul needs greater nourishment than greenbacks to sustain its eternal nature. It is why I left my old life a year ago and have not looked back since.

"Most humans know nothing of true values," Budd continued. "We give all that is finest in us and crush that which is the best in others for the sake of money and power. We barter eternal soul stuff in return for status and transient gain, which, even as we clutch it, melts away. Everything that is physical deteriorates with time. If material wealth and gain are your priorities, than you will only be scaling the peaks of life's illusions as opposed to ascending the summit of eternal Truth. That is the beauty of the example Jesus set. Jesus had the power to conquer an earthly kingdom, but he also had the wisdom to see how paltry and childish such ambitions are. The living treasure of the hearts of men was the kingdom Jesus sought. The kingdom of heaven within each human heart."

Budd's words validated my inner beliefs, my decision to leave a high-paying job and all its perks and venture into the great unknown, using only trust and intuition as my navigational tools. I didn't find great insight camping in the wilderness, but I was definitely receiving a lifetime's worth in one single night in Lander.

"What are the most important things in life?"

"Those which you can take out of this life, such as kindness, charity, patience and unselfishness. The pureness of those actions is anabolic to all of life. And the effect of those positive actions is real. What we do in life echoes in eternity. Even the smallest acts of kindness carry tremendous weight in the spirit world. The teacher who takes the time to encourage a struggling student, the business man or woman who lays aside a work-related matter to come to the aid of a stranger, have chosen the real in favor of the insignificant. They build a positive world rather than destroy it."

"Is there anything in the universe which is indestructible?"

"Love. It passes all sorts of tests with absolute invincibility."

Love. All religions speak of it. All New Age authors advocate its virtues. I turned to look at the Holy Ones who were now sitting peacefully while Freud slept. I had the feeling they were waiting for something, but I wasn't sure what.

"Do you know why they are all here tonight?" Budd asked.

"They are depressed with all that is happening in the world today," I answered. "Their teachings have been misconstrued, their wisdom not used for the good of humanity, scores of humans murdered in the name of religion."

"That is what saddens them, yes. But it is not what brings them here to Lander, Wyoming."

"Why did they come?"

"They came for you."

I was startled. "For me?"

"Yes. Just for you. They have a gift they want to give."

"A gift?"

"A Divine Revelation. One that can forever change the future of this world."

I wasn't sure if I was prepared for this. "That sounds

incredible," were the words that unconsciously sprang from my mouth.

"It is. Let's join them. They are waiting. And I believe you are ready."

We joined the Holy Ones at their table. There was silence for a few moments. Each looked at me with a warm, blissful countenance. I felt awkward. I wasn't sure if they really had a Divine Truth they were willing to divulge or if Jesus was up to another one of His practical jokes. Then, one at a time, they each spoke.

"We came here tonight for a reason," said Jesus.

"Please know what we speak is the Truth," said Buddha.

"We came to tell you that you could be the next mighty Prophet," said Moses.

"What!" I was stunned.

"The next Messiah," added Muhammad.

"The Great Savior of Mankind," proclaimed Jesus.

Their words sounded preposterous, even sacrilegious. I couldn't believe what they were saying.

"Impossible!" I said with skepticism.

"With the power of God, nothing is impossible," remarked Muhammad.

"Or 'Impossible is Nothing'," said Jesus with a smile. "Remember the addidas commercial?"

Surely, they were joking. I scanned their faces. They all seemed quite serious. This was not a joke.

"I am just a mere mortal," I said.

"So was I," said Moses.

"And I," remarked Muhammad.

"And I," added Buddha.

Jesus was conspicuous by His silence. I looked at Him inquisitively, hoping for a reply. None would be forthcoming. He just sat there, motionless, and gently smiled back.

"To believe I can save humanity would be megalomaniacal thinking on my part, wouldn't you think? Really, there is nothing I can do."

"Yes there is," said Jesus.

"I am not powerful, as are you," I argued. "I am not enlightened, like Buddha. Nor do I have the courage to walk the difficult paths that you all walked."

"Not all paths are difficult," said Buddha.

"You don't have to live a life of hardship or persecution," Muhammad remarked.

"Or part the Red Sea," said Moses.

"Or die nailed to a wooden cross," added Jesus.

"The path can be much easier than that," said Buddha.

I was still skeptical. David Sahadi, the world's next Great Savior? Pathetic! Surely, they are delusional, or have mistaken me for someone else. Perhaps they are intoxicated by wine, the high altitude, the thin Wyoming air.

"Alcohol doesn't affect us in the spirit world," said Jesus. "The only intoxicant for us is Love."

"How can I possibly save the world," I asked with cynicism.

"The voice of God is in everyone's heart."

"The angels whisper gently in everyone's ears."

"Open your heart and you shall hear."

Soon they began speaking rapidly, one right after the other, without pausing between statements. Like a tennis fan watching a match at center court at Wimbledon, my head swung back and forth, side to side, trying to make eye contact with The One who was speaking. But it became fruitless. I couldn't keep up. Instead, I decided to stare straight ahead, let my vision lose its focus, and allow my consciousness to fully absorb the profound words being spoken. Soon, their voices blended into each other's, melding as if they were One, one common voice relaying one universal message.

"All you have to do is be kind."

"Loving."

"Compassionate."

"Gentle."

"Forgiving."

"Graceful."

"Understanding."

"Giving."

"With those you meet."

"And especially, with yourself."

"Each for all."

"All for each."

"Work for harmony."

"Work for love."

"Work for the united state of all life."

"The power of God is everywhere."

"It is infinite."

"It is in everything."

"And in every one."

"As without, so within."

"The Power of God expands when you give."

"Give to others."

"Give wholly."

"And give of pure heart."

"Give not with the thought to gain."

"But also know that as you give, so you shall gain."

"The more you give, the more you get."

"And the more you get, the more you can give."

"See everyone in your own self."

"And your own self in everyone."

"God is All-Giving"

"God is Life."

"God is the Creator."

"And He creates constantly."

"God is behind…"

"And through…"

"Everything."

 "From a rock to a man."

"From a planet to a sun."

"All have Life."

"All are part of God."

"God is Love."

"Love is God felt."

"Love others as you would like others to give love unto you."

"Love multiplies as it divides."

"Love given, grows."

"And love hoarded, dwindles."

"It is better to love than be loved."

"The power of God is in you."

"If Love is in your heart."

 "Love is the most powerful force in the universe."

"If you love purely, you have the power to save the world."

"Love cures all."

"Do not be overcome by evil."

"Overcome evil with good."

"Do not fear darkness."

"Darkness is merely the absence of Light."

"As hate is the absence of Love."

"Conquer hate with Love."

"For Love conquers all."

"Just as Light always illuminates Darkness."

"It's Last Call."

"Last Call!"

"Last call for humanity."

"Last Call for alcohol," shouted the bartender.

"Snap out of it."

"Snap out of it, David."

And with a snapping of fingers my trance was broken. I stared straight ahead, bemused and inspired.

"Thought we lost you for a second there," said Jesus.

I looked around the table, at the faces of the prophets, the gods, the enlightened ones. They were all smiling with grace, humility and compassion. Their auras were expansive, interacting, and glowed brightly. I felt as though I, too, was empowered and radiating light.

"Wow!" I said. "It's that simple?"

"It's that simple," they said in unison.

"Seems too easy to be true."

"There is great Truth in simplicity," remarked Buddha.

"Simplicity is very powerful," added Moses.

"Humanity often seeks complex problems to complex solutions," said Muhammad, "when the simplest solution is often the most potent."

"Besides," remarked Jesus, "would I lie to you?"

"And you really think I have it in me to become a biblical messiah?" I posed, intoxicated with wonder and glee.

A look of incredulity appeared on all their faces. Then, they burst with laughter.

"David Sahadi a Biblical Prophet?" chuckled Moses.

"What are you, a megalomaniac?" added Muhammad.

"It appears you still cling tightly to Ego," noted Buddha.

"Do you have a Messiah Complex or something?" quipped Jesus.

Suddenly I went from a great high to a humbled low. I felt foolish, embarrassed, confused.

"Be easy on yourself, David," said Jesus. "We are just teasing."

"The message we give you is not just for you. It is a message we give to all," Muhammad informed.

"Every one has the capability to save mankind," added Jesus.

"To change the world," Buddha said.

"What a beautiful world it could be if everyone heeded the words just spoken."

"Your only mission is to start with you, and hopefully spread love, compassion and reverence to at least one other person in this life."

"Then, my brother, it has a chance to spread like a wildfire."

"You don't need to save the world."

"A country."

"A province."

"A town."

"It all starts with one person."

"Inspire one person and you can save the world."

"Because that one person you inspire might save the world."

"Or that one person might inspire the one person who saves the world."

"Now let us go to the bar and have a nightcap," Jesus suggested. "It really is last call."

With a snort and a startled shake of his head, Sigmund Freud awoke from his deep slumber. He looked around, confused, unsure of the time, unaware of the conversation that just transpired.

"What did I miss?" he asked, hoping for illumination.

"Nothing," replied Budd, taking a sip of the eternal Heineken.

"And everything, too..."

Chapter 9

"LAST CALL FOR alcohol," declared the bartender.

"Or Perrier," quipped Jesus, nudging Muhammad in the arm with his elbow.

We were all gathered around the television, watching the conclusion of the baseball game. It was the bottom of the twelfth. The Red Sox had scored three runs in the top of the inning during the round-table discussion with the Holy Ones. The score was now 11-8. From all accounts it had been a remarkable game. I had missed most of it, but was fortunate enough to have witnessed the dramatic moments. My mind was still processing the depth and simplicity of the Divine Revelation, but I allowed my emotions to embrace my old Yankee passion as The Prophets enthusiastically looked on.

"I'm hoping the Yankees can pull it out," wished Muhammad.

"Then you hope against hope," stated Moses, "because as God is my witness, with prayer and positive thinking, The Curse will be lifted tonight."

"As you think, so shall it be," Buddha remarked.

I turned to Jesus. "Who are you rooting for?" I asked.

"Neither team."

"Do you not like baseball?"

"To the contrary: I truly appreciate the game, the strategy, the drama. But the players and fans of both teams pray to me, so I cannot choose sides."

It appeared as though the game would end without drama. The first two batters for the Yankees both made weak outs. The Red Sox were one out away from burying their demons and advancing to the World Series. It seemed as though The Curse would finally be laid to rest tonight.

"It's OK," said Jesus. "If they lose, think how happy Mose will be. Take solace in his happiness."

"Besides," added Buddha, "it's good to let go of attachment and control your emotions. Never let them be manipulated by a force you cannot control."

Still, I was rooting for the Bronx Bombers to make

another miracle comeback. Two in one night, however, seemed improbable.

And then Hope found me and made its presence known.

The next batter walked. And the batter after that singled sharply to right. Suddenly, the tying run was at the plate in the person of Bernie Williams.

"Go Yanks!" cheered Muhammad.

"Reverse the Curse!" countered Moses.

The first pitch was a fastball that sailed high for ball one. The second was a slow curve taken for a strike. On the third pitch, Bernie Williams hit a slow roller to second. It should have been the final out of the game. But the second baseman momentarily bobbled the ball, recovered, and hurriedly threw to first. His throw pulled the first baseman off the bag. Safe! If the Red Sox were to lose this game, a new rogue was just born in Beantown.

"Not again!" pleaded Moses with a sense of impending doom.

The bases were loaded. The Yankees were down by three runs. Derek Jeter, the Hero of a Hundred Heroics, the All-Star shortstop who sent the game into extra innings with a dramatic two-out home run in the bottom of the ninth, was at bat. He represented the winning run. Fifty-six thousand fans in Yankee Stadium were on their feet screaming. For the first time tonight, the pool tables were quiet and there was no music to be heard. Everyone in the bar was transfixed by the drama unfolding on the screen.

"How fitting," said Muhammad, "that Derek Jeter has the chance to become The Hero once again?"

"How fitting," noted Moses, "that The Hero now has a chance to become The Goat?"

"Go Jeets!" implored Muhammad the Yankee.

"The Curse ends tonight!" countered Moses the Bosox fan.

The Red Sox made a pitching change, bringing in the wily knuckleballer, Tim Wakefield. Twice this series Wakefield had beaten the Yankees as a starter. His pitches seemingly danced in the air, drifting ever so slowly, taunting and teasing the batter the entire sixty feet and six inches to home plate. The Red Sox were hoping Jeter would be over eager and flail mightily at the slow pitch.

Wakefield apparently thought the same thing. He stared at the catcher, Jason Varitek, to get the sign. When he had it, he eased back into the stretch position. He checked the runner at first, then the runner at third for good measure. Not that they were going anywhere. It was all up to Jeter now. After a deep breath, Wakefield got into his motion, and, with every ounce of his being, surprisingly delivered a blazing fast ball to the plate. Jeter took a mighty swing, fouled the ball off his shin, and collapsed in agony at plate. He was in severe pain. The crowd still stood, but now they stood still and silent. Derek Jeter was unable to get up under his own power. Eventually, he was lifted and carried off the field by the trainers.

"Yes!" cheered Moses. "The Curse just got reversed! Jeter is out of the game! Can you say, 'game over'?"

It had been an unbelievable night. Words could not describe the magic and wonder felt, the insight gained. Still, I was now transfixed to the television as if some celestial battle was being waged.

"If you could make one wish right now, what would it be?" Budd asked.

I took an anxious breath. "I know this sounds trivial, especially in light of the events tonight, but I sure wish the Yankees could pull this game out. It would take a minor miracle, I'm afraid."

"Miracles are real, David. So, too, is the power of The Word."

"God's Word?"

"The spoken word," Budd emphasized.

The pinch-hitter for Derek Jeter was a rookie named Kris Chambers. He was called up from the minors just two weeks earlier. I had read an article about him before my camping experience in The Badlands. They called him "Casper" because his skin was white as a ghost. As he walked to the batter's box, I couldn't tell where the white uniform ended and his sleeveless forearms began. This was his first major league at bat. A graphic on the screen informed that he had never hit a home run in his professional career. Not in the rookie leagues, Single A, nor Double A. But the Yankees didn't need a homer here. I was just hoping he had a patient eye and could string out a walk or get an unlikely base hit to keep the inning alive. The dangerous slugger, Gary Sheffield, was on deck. He represented the Yankees' greatest hope.

Just then the door to the bar swung violently open, and I beheld a great vision in white, radiating a bright light. It was Babe Ruth, the Yankee legend, the greatest baseball player of all-time! He was dressed in the Yankees' home uniform: white jersey and pants with midnight blue pinstripes, blue stockings, and an interlocking blue "NY" on his chest. Atop his head he wore the famed blue Yankee cap with a white NY insignia. In his right hand he carried an old, chocolate brown baseball bat that bore a storied history with its countless dents and dings. Moses looked worried. With intense deliberation, Babe Ruth walked to where we were standing, his old cleats making a foreboding echo with each purposeful step on the hardwood floor, his eyes never wavering from the screen. Then he stopped beside me, and, just as he did that glorious September day eighty years ago when he promised a dying boy in a hospital bed that he would hit a home run, he raised his right hand and pointed silently to the heavens.

I turned back to the screen. The Red Sox pitcher delivered his signature knuckle ball. Casper Chambers swung and lofted a harmless fly ball into the air towards right field. Game over. Or so I thought.

At first the outfielder ran in, hoping to catch the easy pop up. But then he stopped. He took one step backwards. Then two. Soon, he started backpedaling. A sudden wind began to howl. The ball kept sailing, further and further into the black New York night, as if the hopes of fifty-six thousand fans, and the ghosts of Gehrig, DiMaggio, Mantle, Maris, Munson, and the venerable legends of Monument Park were all blowing a collective and determined breath, hoping against hope for the ball to clear the outfield wall. The Red Sox right fielder raced back with a sudden urgency. The ball astonishingly continued to sail deep into the dark sky. He went all the way back to the warning track. With his right hand he felt for the padded blue wall. Then he jumped high, his gloved hand extending high above the fence. The ball hit his mitt and popped back out. It bounced high into the air. When it finally descended, it cleared the wall by inches. Home run! The most unlikeliest of heroes, in the most improbable of endings, had just hit a grand slam to give the Yankees a miraculous 12-11 victory and send the Bronx Bombers to the World Series! The delirious crowd screamed with intoxicated frenzy as the players mobbed each other on the lush green infield of The House That Ruth Built. Surely, Casper Chambers would be heralded the next great Yankee legend and be elevated to deity status as the newest god on the streets of New York.

"A miracle!" screamed an ecstatic Muhammad.

"Damn those Yankees! The bloody Curse lives!" cried Moses, as his head dropped despondently into his arms.

And then on the television a little man in blue decided to play god. He was Bruce Jennings, the first base umpire. He had run all the way down the right field line and was now pointing emphatically into the stands and waving his arms. He ruled fan interference. Game still over, but now the Red Sox were declared winners.

"What?!?" I yelled in protest.

"Incredulous!" said Muhammad.

"You've got to be kidding me!" I said in disbelief at the television, and I'm sure the fifty-six thousand fans in Yankee Stadium echoed the same sentiment. The Yankees' skipper, Joe Torre, raced onto the field to argue the call, but there would be no reversal. The only thing reversed were the fortunes of two franchises and their fans, all because of one man's personal judgment. Disbelief turned to solemn shock. The fans were stunned. The Yankees were shocked. And so was I. The Red Sox began to celebrate and rejoice. What was just moments ago a miraculous comeback for the Yankees was now erased and rewritten. History would record this as the biggest choke in sports history. Eighty-six years of misery for the Boston faithful had finally come to an end.

"The Curse is over! It's a miracle!" exclaimed a jubilant Moses.

"We'll get 'em next year," declared Muhammad.

I turned to look at Babe Ruth. How could this be? Just then he unbuttoned his pinstriped-shirt, and, with a young schoolboy's gleam in his eyes, he revealed an old, dirty Red Sox jersey underneath.

"It's from 1918," he said with a proud smile, "the last time the Sox won it all."

I was appalled. "The Babe turns his back on the Yankees?" I protested. "That's sacrilege!"

"Not at all," The Babe replied. "The Curse is real.

I ought to know. And I am a Yankee through and through."

"Then why did your curse not work tonight? And why the change of uniforms?"

"Every eighty six years or so, I try to show a little compassion for my original team, even though they did hurt my feelings when they traded me before my prime. I'm learning to be humble."

"The Curse is dead," I lamented.

"No it's not. Starting next year, another Curse will begin. But I won't torment the Red Sox fans as long this time. Perhaps only fifty or sixty years before they win it again. I am trying to better my spirit, David."

I smiled at the realization that the spirits all liked to play with us mortals living on the physical plane.

"Now buy the Babe a pitcher of beer, will you kid? Unless, of course, you want The Curse of The Bambino to haunt you, too."

While I waited to order The Babe a pitcher of the bubbly golden brew, Jesus indulged Muhammad.

"How about playing a little live music with me to keep the celebration going?" Jesus suggested.

"I don't feel like playing anything right now."

"Come on," Jesus said gingerly. "You'll feel better. Plus, we have a special guest to perform with us tonight."

Muhammad became curious. "Who would that be?"

"Pops."

"Pops? Now you're talking! Ok, let the music begin."

I remained at the bar between Budd and The Babe. Jesus gathered The Others and escorted them to an open area by the jukebox. From behind the music machine He retrieved a guitar case and placed it upon the pool table. He handed Muhammad what appeared to be a brand new Oscar Schmidt acoustic guitar. Then He gave Moses a violin and Buddha a fiddle. Still retrieving instruments from the one seemingly bottomless guitar case, He handed a musical instrument to everyone who wanted to play, fifteen in all, as if he was feeding the mob at Judea with seven loaves of bread. Finally, to my surprise, He introduced the great jazz musician, the legendary Louis Armstrong. "Pops" was in the house! Louis strolled to the front of the assembly and began playing his classic song, *"What A Wonderful World."*

I see skies of blue, and clouds of white
The bright blessed day, dark sacred night
And I think to myself, what a wonderful world

Louis Armstrong was young, radiant, enveloped by a beautiful aura as he sang in his trademark deep, raspy voice. And his cheeks expanded like a puffer belly fish whenever he blew his trumpet.

The colors of the rainbow, so pretty in the sky,
Are also on the faces of people going by
I see friends shaking hands, saying, 'how do you do?'
They're really saying, 'I love you.'

His smile stretched from ear to ear, person to person, spirit to loving spirit. Everyone was smiling, hugging, rocking slowly back and forth with the music, singing along in unison with Louis.

I turned to Budd. "This seems like a pretty cheesy ending to a pretty amazing night."

"Some people like cheese," he said with a genuine smile.

Surrendering to the simple joy of the live performance, I, too, smiled as Armstrong's deep voice bellowed through the tavern, and it seemed as if the beauty of this moment had the capacity to reverberate through all the streets of this small town, through the surrounding mountains and open plains, from one end of this wonderful world to the other.

Chapter 10

THE NEXT MORNING I awoke with a slight headache. It wasn't a hangover. After all, I only had two, maybe three beers the entire night. My brain was simply weary from spinning, twisting and turning like an F-5 tornado all night. But despite the slight physical inconvenience, my spirit was elated. I was infused with abundant joy.

As I pulled onto the road that leads to Yellowstone, I pictured Sigmund Freud sitting beside me, proclaiming my epiphany was a mere hallucination brought on by beer and the absence of dinner. But I knew the events of the previous night were profoundly real. The message was clear and beautiful; it resonated in my soul.

There is a saying that goes, "for those who believe, no explanation is necessary; for those who don't, no explanation will do." That certainly applies here. There would be no one for me to recount the improbable events of that incredible night in a town in the middle of Wyoming named Lander. Nobody would believe me. Yet I know what really happened, the divine forces that were present, the miracles witnessed, the great truths bestowed upon me by the Holy Ones. And I had a new mission in life: I was determined to be grateful for every magnificent moment, to love as well as be loved, to walk the path with grace, humility and compassion, and to try and see the beauty in every blessed soul whose paths crossed mine.

As I continued to drive west along Highway 26, the snow-capped peaks of the Grand Tetons began to emerge from the horizon and kiss the pristine blue sky. Fields of yellow wild flowers danced in the gentle wind, and a still, smiling lake reflected the beauty of the sky above. Rows of dark green poplar and pine spread their branches as if welcoming the warming embrace of the sun, and a huge red-tailed hawk soared effortlessly on the invisible thermals above. I was reminded of God's brilliance. His Divine Presence was everywhere.

Pops was right: what a wonderful world it could be…

ISBN 141208010-X

9 781412 080101